What would you do if you found out your late spouse wasn't the biological parent of your stepchild as they had led you to believe? Would you let it go, in hopes the child wouldn't go looking for their birth family, or would you help them in their search?

This is the dilemma Neil Falcon faces when he first discovers his late wife, Rita, wasn't the biological mother of his teenage stepdaughter, Rikki.

His decision to look for her roots puts them on a path that leads them to a part of Neil's past, one he thought was locked away forever.

Kelsey Wagner is shocked to see the man she once adored appear on her doorstep with claims that Rikki may be her biological child. After finding out her daughter wants her to be a part of her life, she agrees.

Amidst the confusion of raising a teenage daughter, the old feelings resurface. They know their daughter wants them to become a family, but can they make it work?

Away to Me
Copyright © 2019 V.J. Allison
ISBN: 978-1-4874-2651-4
Cover art by Martine Jardin

Published by eXtasy Books Inc or
Devine Destinies, an imprint of eXtasy Books Inc

Look for us online at:
www.eXtasybooks.com or www.devinedestinies.com

Away to Me
Tri-Town Book 1

By

V.J. Allison

DEDICATION

In loving memory of Amber, my beloved writing companion, purring teddy bear, and Monitor Kitty, who left us on August 20, 2018, at the age of 13 years old.

CHAPTER ONE

August
Montreal, Quebec
Kelsey's apartment

K elsey Wagner stared at the papers she was holding in shock. Tears filled her eyes, which blurred the words, making them run together like ink under water.

DNA can show it was someone else.

"Kelsey? Are you okay?" Neil Falcon's question brought her back to the present.

She glanced up at him, a former counsellor from her time in a house for runaway teens, then moved her gaze back to the documents in her hand.

"I'm fine, give me a minute," Kelsey mumbled distractedly, trying to discern what had led Neil and Rikki in her direction. She was barely a high school graduate, but she knew how easily one could be led away from the truth.

Or toward it.

Take a deep breath and look at why he thinks you're the biological mother of his adopted daughter.

She read the birth date.

That's the same.

So was the time of birth, and the hospital in Shelburne, where her daughter was born.

Gender?

There was a photocopy of the card for her bassinet in the hospital, and Kelsey's heart skipped a beat as she recognized the handwriting. *Baby Girl*. The last name was scratched out.

The data showed that Rikki Falcon, Neil's adoptive child, was her biological daughter, the one Kelsey had given up for adoption when she was only sixteen years old.

This can't be real. Neil has his facts mixed up. Rikki isn't mine. She belongs to someone else. My child is in another province, far away from Nova Scotia.

She whispered tearfully, "How sure are you? Everything lines up, but there's still a chance she may not be mine."

"C'mon, Kelsey, you know I wouldn't have come to Montreal if I wasn't sure."

She nodded as she remembered how Neil wasn't one to jump to conclusions—he'd prefer to have concrete proof before he did something that could hurt his adopted child.

It's a thirteen-hour drive from Bridgewater, Nova Scotia. No one drives that far unless they are on vacation or have pressing business to tend to.

"I know," she whispered.

He awkwardly shifted and stared down at her with concern. "If you don't want to know, I understand, but think of Rikki. When she found out she was adopted, she wanted to know who her real parents were. When things started pointing in your direction, she was over the moon."

Kelsey shook her head, still unable to believe it. "I'm not the only teenager who gave birth to a girl that day," she reminded him. There had been two others, but one girl was only fourteen, and the other was eighteen. She had been the only sixteen-year-old in the maternity ward that week.

"I double-checked in case I was wrong. You're the same age, and you gave birth at the right time on her birthday. Everything else lines up for it to be you," he shot back.

Kelsey's gut was telling her that although the records could have been mixed up in his search, Neil's findings were correct, and his stepdaughter was her biological child.

She straightened to her full height and met his deep brown-eyed gaze. "When and where do you want me to take the test?"

Neil visibly relaxed at her question. "The lab said you can drop by at any time today, and we'll know within twenty-four to thirty-six hours. Rikki has already given them her sample. All they have to do is compare it to yours."

"And if she is my daughter? What happens then?" she asked.

"Don't think about it right now. We'll deal with it after the results come back, okay?" His fingers brushed her cheek.

The soothing gesture stirred up so many memories. "One step at a time." She shook her head in amazement and smiled sadly.

He chuckled and returned the smile. "Are you going to be okay?"

"I think so. We don't know for sure, so there's no point in getting excited or upset until it's proven one way or another."

"Right." He glanced at his watch and sighed. "I'd better get back to the hotel before Rikki starts wondering where I am."

At her door, Neil stared down at her for a moment. "Call me if you need me, or if you just need to talk, okay?"

She nodded, and they exchanged a sad smile before he left.

Kelsey slumped against the wall and stared at the door for a long time after his departure, the disbelief, her past, and the future colliding in a supernova.

He hasn't changed at all. He's still the leader, the rock for anyone who needs one. He let me lean on him more times than I can remember.

Neil had pulled Kelsey out of the darkness and showed she wasn't white trash, just a lost soul in need of guidance. If she hadn't met him, she would have died on the streets on her path of self-destruction, another anonymous statistic.

Neil Falcon had saved her life.

Because of that, she developed a hero-worship for him that

had deepened into something else.

I fell for him, hard.

Neil backed his half-ton pickup into a parking space. He had gotten lost on his way back to his hotel, his mind too focused on the events of the last six months to follow the map on the seat beside him.

Up until the past winter, Rikki hadn't known she was adopted. She, like he, believed the woman who'd raised her was her birth mother. His late wife, Rita Hunter Falcon, had never mentioned anything about it. She and Neil had been trying to have another child when her stage four cervical cancer had been diagnosed.

They'd found the papers hidden in an old leather box at the back of his and Rita's closet. The front of the envelope had the name and address of a lawyer's firm on it.

Inside were several papers, including Rita's will. One was an adoption certificate for a girl, dated three days after Rikki's birthday. Other papers were related to Rita and her first husband, Brandon, taking full custody and parental responsibility for a child who was named Clarissa Dawn Banacheck.

Another was a birth certificate with the birth parents' names blacked out. Neil had tried to see if he could make out either name, but whoever did it had scratched over the names with an instrument to hide the original creases made by a pen. The only things on the original were the child's birth name, time, birthday, weight and length.

The last paper, a handwritten note from her father, Brandon Hunter, was the final piece of evidence. It was dated a month before he died in an accident, when Rikki was two months old.

My dear Erika Lynn,
If you are reading this, that means you have found your adoption

papers. It wasn't my choice to keep this from you. It was Rita's. She wanted you to believe that she was your birth mother, so you wouldn't have fantasies about the people who gave you to us.

Please, look for your birth family when the time is right. They deserve to see what a delight you are. I love you, my darling daughter.

Your adoptive dad, Brandon.

Neil had been shocked to see it all in print.

Rita Hunter Falcon was not Rikki's birth mother.

Rikki hadn't known because Rita had never told her.

She hadn't told Neil about it either.

If she lied to him about Rikki being her biological child, what else had she kept secret?

Like being infertile? Jesus.

Those questions might never be answered. Rita had died almost two years ago. She and Rikki were from New Brunswick and had moved to Halifax, Nova Scotia three months before Neil met her, eleven years ago.

It was a month after their discovery that Rikki decided she wanted to find out where she came from and asked for his help.

At first, Neil had been reluctant to do it. Sometimes the birth parents didn't want anything to do with the child they had given up years ago. It would hurt his daughter if that happened to her. Neil refused to be part of anything that could put Rikki in harm's way.

When Rikki's grades slipped from C's to D's after Rita's death, he believed Rikki needed a distraction. They'd begun the search for her birth family.

It took several months to find her biological mother. The adoption lawyer's firm refused to open their records without Rita's permission. However, they gave them the name of the social worker who had taken Rikki's case.

That was another dead end. Due to confidentiality laws,

the records were sealed until Rikki's eighteenth birthday. They would only be opened before that if either of her birth parents allowed it in writing.

Neil had started spending hours reading various birth records in their county and others in the western half of the province, without success.

It wasn't until he checked the records in Shelburne County that they had a possibility, six months after they had discovered that manila envelope. The date, time, weight, and everything else lined up with Rikki's original certificate of birth.

It was the name of a person that had shaken his world.

Kelsey Bernice Wagner.

It can't be the same one, he'd frantically thought as the words in front of his vision spun in circles. *This has to be a mistake!*

He glanced between the papers and the records. His stomach churned when he saw the mother's birth date line up perfectly with a teenager he had known over a decade ago.

He had stared at the screen and tried not to let shock overtake him.

The woman who once held his heart in his hands had given birth to his little girl.

Rikki pounced on him the instant he walked into the hotel room.

He hugged her and motioned her to sit on the bed so they could talk.

"Is Kelsey going to do it?" she asked.

Neil nodded distractedly. "Yeah."

"And?"

"She wants to wait to until we know either way before we do anything."

"Okay." Her voice was small and sad, and he could tell she was fighting tears.

"Hey," he said softly and put his arm around her

shoulders, "don't think about it until we know for sure."

Rikki sniffled. "If she isn't my real mom, would you mind if I talked to her anyway?"

"I'll allow it, if Kelsey agrees. I know you liked her the last time you saw her."

"Dad, you knew her a long time ago. How did you meet her?"

So, the questions were starting again. Rikki's list was unending, and although he didn't want to answer some of them, maybe it was the right time. If Kelsey turned out to be her birth mother, Rikki should know a few things.

Kelsey's childhood had been dysfunctional at best—even more than his—and she was lucky to be alive.

If Kelsey turned out to be her birth mother, it would also give Rikki closure on why she was given up for adoption. If she wasn't, it would explain to Rikki why Kelsey seemed a little distant around people she didn't know, and more open with him.

"We met at a shelter for runaway teens in Halifax, where I was working at the time. She was a resident."

"She ran away from home?"

Neil felt a stab of pain as he recalled the first time he saw Kelsey. "She was brought in by a social worker after spending two days in the hospital. Her mother had beaten her within an inch of her life. When her mother passed out after drinking that evening, Kelsey snuck out of the house. She stole her mother's car and drove two hours before she had to stop."

Rikki stared up at him with wide eyes. "Why didn't she keep going?"

"Adrenaline and fear can only take you so far before the pain hits," Neil replied. "Her mother had twisted her arm so hard behind her back that it snapped in three spots. Her mother had broken a few of Kelsey's ribs before she was finished, and god knows what else. It was amazing Kelsey could drive, let alone that far."

"Wow."

You don't know half of it. Kelsey was a bloody, bruised body, unable to speak much or do a lot for herself due to the injuries. He had checked on her through the first night she was there, to be sure she made it through the night without bad dreams or too much pain. He was sickened to see what a human could do to their own child.

I wanted to protect her, more than the others. She seemed so vulnerable, so broken.

"When I first saw her, I didn't know what she looked like. Her face was swollen and purple, and she could barely see out of one eye. The other one had a scratched cornea, so it was taped shut while it healed."

He turned his head to stare down at Rikki. "It wasn't all physical. Her mother said some nasty things to her over the years, stuff a normal mother would never say to their kid."

"Oh."

"I found out she had given a child up for adoption after she opened up to me. She was scared her mother was going to hurt her child, or that she was going to turn out the same way." He shook his head and scoffed. "I never thought we'd be looking at her as being your birth mom."

He brushed a tendril of straight brown hair out of Rikki's eyes. "Are you sure you want her to be a part of your life if she is your birth mom? I want you to be certain on this, Rikki. Once the results come in, and if she becomes sort of a stepmother to you, there's no turning back."

Rikki played with the hem of her t-shirt.

She always does that when she's nervous.

"I'm sure, Dad. I want to know her, even if it's just her name, that way I'm not always wondering."

He nodded. "We'll work everything out once we know for sure. If she is your mother, I hope you're happy."

"I am."

"That's all I wanted to know."

"I still don't know why Mom didn't tell us."

I'd like to know that, too. Why didn't Rita tell me she wasn't able to have children? We could have adopted another child or gotten a surrogate. "I think she was only doing what she thought was best for you and didn't want to hurt you. You were the best thing in her life."

Rikki started to cry. "I miss her, a lot."

Neil's throat closed. "I miss her too. There are still nights that I'll reach out to hug her, then I realize she isn't. It hurts so much that I can't breathe, knowing she's no longer here," he choked out, hugging Rikki tightly. "When she died, she left a huge hole, not just in your life, but mine too."

He wiped tears off his daughter's cheeks and whispered, "She promised to always be with us, even if we couldn't see her. Remember that."

"It still hurts, Dad."

He kissed her forehead. "I know. We adjust to it after a while, but it never really goes away. Hang on to the good times with her and try to smile sometimes. I don't have plans to leave you for a very long time."

"Love you, Dad."

"You're my whole heart, Rikki."

She nodded and hugged her dad fiercely. Neil prayed that wherever their journey to find his daughter's roots took them, it would lead to joy instead of pain and suffering.

Two days later, Neil picked up the DNA results and drove to Kelsey's apartment so they could read them together without Rikki under foot.

Kelsey's entire body shook and impatience rose in her gut as Neil fumbled with the seal on the envelope. The rasp of paper against paper tore through her ears, and a shimmer of dread went up her spine as Neil silently read the results.

"What does it say?" she prompted quietly after a moment.

He let out a long sigh. "It's a girl," he said and cleared his throat.

She took the papers from his hand and scanned the page, unable to believe it.

She read the results, and tears formed in her eyes.

Rikki is my child.

Her gaze rose to meet his, and they stared at each other tearfully. When he motioned to her, Kelsey flew into his embrace. Her feet left the floor for a moment as Neil hugged her.

She scrambled to put everything in its place.

Rikki was the baby she only saw twice, once right after she was born and for a half hour the day after. She had held the little girl and given her a bottle. When the nurse came to take her to her adoptive parents, Kelsey had hugged her tightly, told her she loved her, and gave her one last kiss.

Kelsey thought it was going to be the only memories she would have of her child.

I never thought I'd see her again. Holy shit.

"What are we going to do now?" her soft question broke the silence.

Neil let out a long breath. "I'm not sure," he replied, "but if you want her, I won't stop you."

His words felt like lava to her ears, hot, uncomfortable, and unwelcome.

Say what?

She straightened to stare at him. "What do you mean by that?" She couldn't keep the annoyance out of her voice.

"Kelsey, she's your daughter. I'm only her stepfather, and the courts think the biological parents should raise—" He coughed.

Her eyes widened. "You think I'm going to fight you for custody."

He averted his gaze.

10

"I can't believe you think I would be mean enough to sep-
arate you two!" She pulled out of his arms, stomped a few feet
away from him, and bit her lip.

Fucking asshole. He knows me better than that!

"You're her mother. I know how hard it was for you to give
her up. I lost track of how many times you cried on my shoulder because you missed her, that's why I thought—" He
shoved his hands into his jean pockets as he turned away
from her.

She's his kid. I'd rather gargle acid than hurt him, or Rikki.

When she saw his hunched shoulders, stiff back, and shaking knees, Kelsey's fury at him turned to understanding and
sorrow. She sniffled and swiped at some tears with her sleeve
before she reached out to touch his arm. "Neil, look at me."

He shook his head, his entire body tense.

She cupped his cheek and forced him to face her. Her
thumb caressed his cheekbone, and she pressed her forehead
against his while she tried to explain her feelings about what
was right for Rikki. "She's your kid, more than she'll ever be
mine. You're the only dad she remembers, and I'd hurt both
of you if I took her from you. I don't want to do that."

He nodded reluctantly and sighed. His arms went around
her waist.

She slid her arms around him and held him close.

He's shocked and confused like I am.

We are a team, if Rikki wants both of us.

"Do you want visitation?" Neil asked softly after a few
minutes.

She pulled back and stared up at him. "I'd love it, but I'd
rather not intrude."

"She wants you in her life, and I do too. We'll make ar-
rangements for you to see her during vacations and holidays."

"I want to get a lawyer to help us set things up. That way
you know where you stand, and we know what's expected

from all of us."

"Kelsey, I trust you—"

"I don't want you thinking I'll go back on my word and take off with her sometime." She peered up at him and blinked.

"Once you give your word, it's written in stone."

She fingered his shirt collar. "I also want to pay child support."

He stiffened. "Rikki and I don't need your money."

"It's right and fair, Neil. You'd be doing the same if things were the other way around."

"Yeah, I would," he grumbled, and let out a long sigh.

"Take it and shut up."

He rolled his eyes.

She chuckled softly.

"This feels weird," she whispered after a moment.

"What does?"

"Having a child with you."

He pulled back to stare at her blankly.

"What?" she asked, exasperated.

"You make it sound like it's a bad thing."

"You're the last person I thought I'd have a kid with," she replied with a wry smile.

He scoffed. "Yeah, considering things."

"Weird or not, I like it. You love her, a lot, and you're doing a great job with her."

Neil let out a long breath. "She's my world."

"And you're hers," she said softly. "If I turn out to be half the parent you are, I'm going to be a great mother."

"Dad!"

Neil grinned when he heard Rikki's voice in the hotel lobby. Apparently, she couldn't wait to hear the news either.

He hugged her hard and placed a kiss on top of her head. Her curiosity had electrified the air so much, he could almost see the jagged lines surrounding her.

She's a great kid. I hope Kelsey can see that and help me teach Rikki how to be a responsible, friendly adult.

Rikki's eyes were wide when she asked, "Did we pass or fail?"

Neil cupped her cheek in his hand gave her a sad smile. "We passed."

Rikki grinned. "We found my birth mom?"

Neil sighed. "I hope you're happy with this."

"I am, Dad!"

She's the light of my life. I hope, in time, she becomes the light of Kelsey's life too.

"She's here. Do you want to say hello to her?"

Rikki pulled out of his embrace and turned. Her face lit up when she saw Kelsey a few feet away.

She slowly walked over to them and stopped in front of her newfound daughter.

"Hi, Kelsey," Rikki said with a grin.

"Hey, Rikki. It's good to see you." She touched the girl's hair awkwardly and bit her lip. "I don't know if I should hug you or–"

Rikki grabbed Kelsey in a bear hug.

Kelsey's gaze met Neil's over the top of their daughter's head. There were tears in her eyes. "Thank you," she mouthed.

Whew. They're happy.

I was terrified they'd be pissed about the results, or Kelsey would want full custody.

Visitation is perfect, if they want it. I'll give Kelsey my number so she can talk to Rikki any time they want to chat, or if she has any questions.

Hurdle one passed.

On to the next challenge, whatever it'll be.

"Kelsey, how many times do I have to say I don't want anything from you?" Neil muttered in exasperation.

"And how many times do I have to tell you I want to help with Rikki?" she shot back angrily.

"There's no need to yell at each other," the lawyer, Maurice Patterson, injected. "Ms. Wagner wants to pay a small stipend each month to help with Rikki's expenses."

"Kelsey makes less a year than I do. It's not right for her to be taking money out of her paycheck to help me!" Neil snapped.

"It's for Rikki, so I can afford it."

"I don't care. We don't need it," he bellowed. He was pissed that she refused to back down. Taking money from her didn't feel right. Kelsey was barely able to pay her rent, let alone child support.

"God, you are stubborn! Take the damn money and shut up."

The aging lawyer let out a sigh and patted Kelsey's arm.

Neil felt the lawyer's watery blue eyes turn to him.

"I suggest you take it, Mr. Falcon, just to keep the peace."

Fuck. She's got the lawyer telling me to take it. Fine, I'll do it, but I'll pay her back, eventually.

Even more annoyed, Neil let out a long, exasperated sigh and flopped down on a chair. "It's going into her college fund."

"That's fine, you are using it for Rikki."

Another short argument about the amount ensued, with Kelsey trying to give more than Neil was willing to allow.

Finally, they settled on a sum that wasn't much lower than what Kelsey said she could send each month.

Neil reluctantly accepted it with a glare.

Hoodwinked, he thought, and picked up his copy of the contract. *Or was it pussy whipped?*

Either way, Neil realized he had been shoved into a corner.

I fucking hate it.

"Neil?"

He stopped ten feet from his truck without turning and snapped, "What?"

"Nothing," she replied.

Neil's anger at her subsided when he heard the regret in her voice.

Me and my big mouth. I don't need her pissed off at me. We have to be friends for Rikki's sake.

He sighed and called over his shoulder, "Kelsey, wait a second."

Her footsteps halted and they turned to face each other across eight feet of asphalt.

"Sorry," he mumbled.

Kelsey took three steps toward him. "I'm sorry too," she whispered.

"You're looking out for Rikki, like a mother should," he replied.

They exchanged a somber smile. She slowly ambled to his side.

When tears started to form in Kelsey's eyes, Neil held her tightly as she sobbed on his shoulder.

"Sorry," she sniffled after a few minutes, "I think I've cried more over the last week than I have in the last year."

"I understand," he said soothingly and rocked her back and forth. "It's been one hell of a wild ride, between finding out Rikki is ours and everything else."

She chuckled wryly. "Ours. I'm still getting used to the idea of having a child with you."

"Is it really that bad?"

"No, and it's feeling less weird each time I think about it." She lifted her head and stared up at him. "I'd rather have you as her dad than anyone else."

A warm tingle traveled up his spine and he grinned.

"Ready to go see our girl?"

She nodded with a tearful smile. "Our girl. I love the sound of that."

"I do too," Neil said and walked her to her car.

CHAPTER TWO

Mid-September

Kelsey called Neil's house in Bridgewater, Nova Scotia
"Hey, Kelsey. Guess what? I aced the math test," Rikki
chirped into the phone.

"That's great, sweetheart. Didn't your dad and I say you
could do it?"

"Yeah, you did," Rikki admitted sheepishly.

Kelsey could picture the girl's grin. *Her smile lights up a*
room.

"You normally call on Wednesdays, why are you calling
on a Monday?"

"Something came up. Is your dad around?"

Rikki sighed dramatically. "You two are going to talk
about me, aren't you? That's the only reason why you want
to talk to him. I'm almost fourteen, and I can make a few de-
cisions for myself."

"Not until you're eighteen years old, and you know your
dad. He won't let you do much unless you're not living with
him," Kelsey replied around a snicker. *Dear god, she sounds so*
much like me.

Rikki growled in reply.

"None of that, unless you want me telling your dad you're
nagging me to let you dye your hair."

Another long, dramatic moan echoed over the airways.
"I'll go get him so you two can keep me locked in this prison."

"It's not that bad, is it? Your father and I are only looking out for you."

"I don't have any fun."

"That's weird, because your father was telling me the other day that you and Taffy landed in the principal's office again. What on earth possessed you to cover Mr. Granger's car with wet toilet paper?"

Rikki snickered.

"Erika Lynn Falcon, you know better than to do something like that."

"He was mean to Taffy by giving her a D, when she aced the damn math test."

"It wasn't really about that, was it? I know he's your least favourite teacher — it was still wrong."

"I get it. Stop ragging me about it."

Kelsey heard someone clear their throat. Her insides tingled happily in anticipation. She always looked forward to hearing his voice, even for a moment.

"Hi, Kelsey."

"Hey, Neil. Something has come up. I can't see you two at the end of the month."

"Let me guess, your boss won't let you have that weekend off." He sounded pissed.

He thinks it happened again, like it's happened the majority of the weekends since the DNA test came back. He hates my boss, for a good reason.

She was fed up with the housecleaning job. It was time to move on.

"No. Rikki can see me out there. I handed in my two-week notice at work."

Silence crackled over the airway for a moment. "Did you find another job?"

"Not yet. I'm hoping for something, soon. Um, there's also a change of address, but I'm not sure exactly what it is yet."

"You're moving? Where?"

"Home."

"Why?"

Kelsey sighed. "I want to see her more than three or four times a year. I hate living so far away from her."

"You don't feel like a real mother to her."

"Yes. I won't move over there unless it's okay with you. You're her main parent—"

"Kelsey, relax. Pack your stuff and get down here. We'll help you set up."

"Are you sure? I don't want to be a bother."

"You know Rikki hates living so far away from you."

"That's true. I don't like living in another province, either. It's time to come home."

"Call us when you're on the way."

"Definitely."

With a long, happy sigh, Kelsey turned her phone off. *I'm wanted.*

Two weeks later

Kelsey popped her head into the larger of two bedrooms in her newly rented house. It was just outside of town limits and only a short walk from Neil and Rikki's home, on the north side of Bridgewater, Nova Scotia. Rikki could take the same bus route to either residence on her way home from school. It had been a lucky find, and Kelsey was grateful it was in her budget and had two bedrooms, one of which she planned to set up for her daughter.

She was lucky to get it. Neil had talked to the owner after noticing the last tenants moving a week earlier. The man was happy to have someone moving in almost right away, and let Neil sign the lease in Kelsey's stead.

She absently caressed the wood of the door frame, happy to be home in Nova Scotia.

"Kelsey, where do you want this?" Rikki called from the hallway.

19

She eyed the box of books Rikki was pointing to, and with a shake of her head, sighed, "Shove them into the bottom of my closet and I'll sort them out later." At her daughter's downcast look, she amended, "Or, we can go through them next weekend while you're here."

Rikki beamed at her and pushed the box into the closet.

Kelsey snickered. Like her, Rikki was a bookworm, and always seemed to be reading when she wasn't on her phone, talking to friends or texting someone.

Today was the exception. Rikki and her best friend, Taffy, had come over to set up Rikki's room and to give Kelsey company while the movers finished bringing her belongings inside the house.

"Miz Wagner? We have your couch here!" one of the men bellowed from the entryway.

"Be right out," Kelsey replied, and ran out into the main area.

As the confusion had her jumping from one place to another, she realized she hated moving, especially from one province to another.

That's it, I'm buying a house once I find one that I can afford. Kelsey scooped up the box of kitchen utensils and plopped it down on the counter. She reached into her back pocket and growled loudly when she realized the scissors she was using to cut tape had disappeared.

Something hit her shin. With a startled yelp, she looked down to see Punky, Neil and Rikki's corgi, staring up at her with a long piece of tape dangling from the side of his mouth and his bum wiggling in excitement as he tried jumping upwards, into her arms.

"Tape isn't good for dogs, Punky, you know that." Kelsey reached down to take it from him.

The chubby dog stared at her happily as she patted him on the head before she moved her fingers to the underside of his jaw. Just as she felt the tape along the back of her hand,

Punky's eyes widened. He shoved at her legs with his front paws, and wriggled away from her.

Startled by how fast a short dog could move, Kelsey let out a soft yelp as she jumped backwards.

"I can see why Neil calls you a chowder head," she grumbled at his retreating bum as he scampered into the living room. She brushed her hands down the front of her denim clad thighs and shook her head.

A chuckle from behind made her jump again. She shot Neil a dirty look and went back to looking for her scissors.

"What did that goof do this time?" he asked as he set a box on the counter.

"Not much, other than scaring the daylights out of me." She shifted the box of utensils and sighed. "I don't think he likes me too much. He's been doing nothing but drive me nuts since he walked in the door."

He handed her a box cutter. "He loves you, Kelsey. I think you're not sure if you like him yet, so he's doing his best to show you he likes you by trying to play with you. Give him a chance, and he'll be your best friend."

"I have, and got thanked for my efforts to become friends with him when he tried running me over when I saw him with something that could hurt him." She opened the box and handed the small knife to Neil before she started setting its contents on the counter. "I don't care if he's Rikki's dog or not, he has to learn to behave while he's here on weekends, else he'll be confined to her room."

He snickered and started helping her organize the heavier kitchen items, their silent comradery soothing to Kelsey's frazzled nerves.

I could get used to this.

A few hours later, Kelsey walked into her room and sat down with a tired sigh.

"Hey Kelsey!" Rikki's voice echoed down the hallway.

She cringed. *Now what?* She was exhausted from the confusion amidst getting unpacked and organizing, in between getting run over by two excited teenagers. If anything else went off kilter, she was going to rip her hair out. "Yeah?"

"Taffy's moms are here to pick her up, and they want to meet you."

Kelsey let out a long, tired breath and flopped onto her back. She was exhausted, filthy and wasn't in the mood for company, nor was she up to meeting the esteemed parents of her daughter's best friend.

However, politeness overruled her tiredness and she stood up with another long sigh. "I'll be out in a minute." She finger-combed her hair into place and hoped she wasn't too dirty from digging in boxes all day.

When she entered the living room, she saw two blond-haired ladies talking with Neil.

The shorter of them grinned and held out a hand. Kelsey noted the resemblance between her and Taffy and assumed this was the girl's mother.

"Hi, Kelsey, I'm Gina, and this is Ruby, my wife." She gestured to the other lady, who smiled and waved.

Small talk about her move was made, along with a few comments on the mischief the dog and girls created while the movers were unloading the truck. Finally, Gina declared it was time to go so Kelsey could get some rest and settle into her new home.

After she and Ruby had gathered up Taffy and shooed her outside, Gina turned to Kelsey and said, "If you want to know anything about Rikki and Taffy, need to talk or even just vent, feel free to call Ruby and I anytime, or come over. We'll bitch about the perils of our kids over coffee."

"Thank you, but I don't want to be a bother."

Ruby shushed Kelsey with a wave of her hand. "You won't be. Gina and I know how tough it is to raise a teenage girl, and we'll be happy to show you the ropes. We parents have to stick together."

Kelsey smiled and nodded. She liked the two women, and she was happy they were including her in their circle. "Thank you."

They grinned at her in reply and with a final wave, exited.

Kelsey smirked after the door banged shut. "I like them."

Neil chuckled. "Yeah, they're great. They've helped me a lot with Rikki, especially after her mom got sick, and in the years since."

"It's really nice of them to offer advice, I'm going to need all the help I can get." She flopped down on the couch with a tired sigh. "It's not every day that you have a teenage daughter appear out of nowhere, and I'm not sure how to be a great mom to Rikki."

He sat down beside her and put a hand on her shoulder. "I think you're doing just fine."

"I wasn't here at all, and you were the one taking care of her while all I did was help you decide on what to do with her sometimes and talk to her on the phone twice a week. Being a mom is a different story." She rubbed her temples and shook her head. "I'm scared I'm going to do something wrong."

"Kelsey, stop worrying. You're going to do fine. I'm learning as I go too, because she changes and grows all the time and I don't know how to take it sometimes. One minute, she's the angel she was at ten, and the next, I'm looking at a young woman who is trying to find her place in the world and telling me I don't know shit. It's not easy, and although it's the toughest job in the world, I wouldn't give it up for anything."

"I hope so, because if I don't do this right, she's going to be scarred for life. I don't want history to repeat itself."

Neil's arms slid around her shoulders. "Stop thinking you're going to turn into your mom. I don't see you treating her the way your mother neglected you. You're already ahead of the game by loving her."

Her head dropped to his shoulder. "True."

"It'll come to you naturally. Just go with the flow, follow my lead, and you'll be fine."

Punky zoomed through the living room, followed by a giggling Rikki.

Kelsey let out a long sigh. "Now what is that blasted dog up to?"

Neil stood up. "Rest. I'll take care of it."

Kelsey leaned into the soft couch cushions with her eyes closed after he followed the pair out of the room. It had been a long day, and the thought of reading a book with a mug of tea in a hot bath was appealing.

So was sleeping round the clock.

She jumped and let out a soft squeal of surprise when something wet and cold touched her bare arm. Her eyes popped open, and she felt something wriggling beside her.

Punky was trying to hide behind her, another piece of tape in his mouth and his big brown eyes blinked at her.

Her gaze narrowed. "You little stinker, you're being naughty again." She slowly started reaching for the tape without moving her gaze from his. "One second," she murmured soothingly, in hopes to get the sticky stuff out of his mouth.

Punky stared at her with a doggy grin.

Her fingers brushed the tape.

His tan ears went back, and he quickly dived off the couch.

Kelsey went face first into the cushions.

"Chowder head," she muttered at the dog's retreating hindquarters.

"I'll get him, Kelsey!" Rikki called and ran down the hallway.

Neil leaned against the archway and started laughing.

"It's not funny!"

"Want to bet? That idiot did the same thing to me a lot over the years."

Kelsey flipped him the finger and flopped back into the cushions with a sigh. "I hope he doesn't pull off any more stunts tonight, I'm too damn tired to chase him."

"Rikki will try to keep him in line." Neil sat down beside her again. "Maybe it wouldn't hurt to take an afternoon and have you getting him to do a few tricks with Rikki and me supervising. That way he knows you like him, too."

"Yeah, sure, you just want to see me go face first into a mud puddle," she grumbled.

He snickered. "We'll make sure there are no puddles."

Kelsey nodded tiredly and closed her eyes.

His arm nudged hers. "We'll clear out so you can get some sleep. It's been a long day."

"You don't have to. I have to get used to the confusion."

"Kelsey, you're dead on your feet. Go get some rest, and we'll see you tomorrow."

Bed sounds amazing. I'd love a bath, but I'm so tired. I'll have one in the morning. Too exhausted to argue, she nodded reluctantly.

After Neil rounded up a protesting Rikki and Punky, Kelsey flopped down on her bed.

Before she fell into slumber, she wondered again if she was doing the right thing with her life and Rikki's.

CHAPTER THREE

K elsey found a job less than a week after moving into her new home. It was at a gas station, and she worked at lot of weekends. After she showed her upcoming schedule with Neil, they decided to ease into Rikki spending nights at her house during the week. She could be there for evenings if Kelsey worked a day shift or was off.

It was during her third week of working that she started to stop in to see her daughter on her way home from working a day shift, with Neil's approval.

She sat on one of the kitchen chairs and sighed gratefully when he gave her a cup of decaf coffee.

"I take it things were nuts?" he asked and sat down across from her.

Kelsey nodded tiredly. "People don't get that I am not the one that decides if gas prices go up or down," she muttered, "If they want to complain to someone about it, they should write or call the review board." She cursed some of the ruder customers a few times and with a long sigh, shook her head.

His reply was cut off by Rikki barging in.

"Hi, Kelsey." Rikki gave her a quick kiss on the cheek and opened the fridge.

"Are you finished with your homework?" Neil asked.

"Not yet, can I finish it after supper?"

"Rikki, you know the rules—"

"I was helping Taffy with hers."

"Helping? How much help were you really giving her?" he asked.

"Dad," Rikki moaned.

"Rikki, listen to your father. Go finish it now, else you're going to lose your phone for the rest of the night," Kelsey said firmly.

She received a glare in reply.

Rikki grumbled something under her breath and rolled her eyes before she left the kitchen.

They discussed her upcoming schedule. Kelsey tried not to, but she yawned a few times during the exchange.

"Do you want me to run you home?" Neil asked.

She shook her head. "I can drive that far." She tried to hold back another yawn without success.

"Kelsey, go home. You're exhausted."

"I promised Rikki that I'd stay for a bit," she protested softly.

"She'll understand, once she sees how tired you are."

"I don't care if I'm tired or not. I want to spend some time with my daughter."

"Did you eat anything today?"

"No, it was too busy, and I forgot to pack a lunch."

"Skipping a meal is a good way to drain your tank," he said. "Go home, get changed, and relax. Rikki and I will be over in a bit."

She eyed him warily. "Why?"

"You want to spend time with Rikki. You need to eat. We'll get something and meet you at your place. We'll stay a while so you two can visit, and you won't have to drive."

It was perfect, Kelsey concluded, although she didn't want to impose on Neil's generosity. He had been flexible with her schedule and letting her stop in on her way to or from work to see their daughter, even though it hadn't been written into their custodial agreement. "I was going to grab a sandwich and pass out on the couch after I got home."

"Now you don't have to do that," he said, "You can relax

and go right to bed after Rikki and I clear out."

She nodded reluctantly. "Give me twenty minutes to go home and change."

"I'll call your favourite pizza joint for a pickup."

When he stood up, she gave him a stern look and said, "Neil, I'm only doing this because I'm too bushed to argue. I'm not making a habit of this."

He put a hand on her shoulder. "I wouldn't have offered if I didn't want to do it."

"I know," she whispered and covered his hand with hers. "But you've done so much by letting me see Rikki whenever I wanted. I feel like I'm taking advantage of you."

"You're not. She wants to see you a lot too, and it would be selfish of me to stop it. She loves you, Kelsey, more than you know."

"I can't help but love her, she's a great kid," she sniffled.

Neil smiled and squeezed her shoulder. "Yeah, she is."

An hour later, they sat around Kelsey's coffee table, picnic style, with an empty pizza box, napkins and plates strewn around them.

"Does Punky like cats?" Kelsey asked.

"As a rule, most corgis do, but he hasn't been around a cat since we adopted him," Neil replied, with trepidation crawling up his spine. "Why?"

"I was thinking about getting a cat from the shelter. I love cats, and I'd love one for company. They're independent and can stay home all day without having to go outside to use the bathroom."

"Punky is going to be here a lot too," Rikki said, and put her arm around the dog.

Kelsey sighed and leaned against the couch. "I get lonely on the nights you and Punky aren't here, sweetheart," she explained, "and I thought it would be okay to adopt another pet. I won't get another dog, because of Punky. I do think of him too."

"He's not going to like it," Rikki warned, "He likes having all of the attention."

"Well, boo-hoo for him, because I want a cat, and I'm going to adopt one tomorrow," Kelsey stated stubbornly.

Neil exchanged a knowing look with Rikki.

I know, she's being stupid. We'll let her find out on her own. He winked at Rikki.

"Don't come crying to me when he retaliates after he meets the cat," he said to Kelsey.

She waved it off. "He'll be fine. Punky is going to love having a kitty to play with. Isn't that right, chowder head?" she cooed.

"This should be interesting," Neil muttered to his daughter.

They exchanged a grin.

Kelsey adopted two cats from the local shelter, Sammy and Casey. Although they were a little skittish at first, the cats slowly adjusted to Punky over the next month. There were some wild moments with the cats, thanks to Punky trying to play with them, but they soon became close pals.

Meanwhile, their respective humans settled into a routine.

Kelsey automatically stopped at Neil's house on her way home from working a day shift, and sometimes on her days off, he was at her place with Rikki. It was easier to talk about things to do with their daughter face to face than over the phone, so she could talk to them about upcoming events— like dances or parent teacher meetings—at once instead of separately.

The memories of how she felt about him long ago started

rearing their heads during that time. She shoved them away with a firm reminder that if it wasn't for Rikki, she wouldn't be living in Nova Scotia and wouldn't be so close to him.

As the holidays approached, Rikki dropped a few hints about what she wanted for Christmas—waking up in the morning with both of her parents there.

Kelsey hesitated, because she felt it would be pushing the limits of Neil's generosity with their daughter. Spending time together during the daytime was one thing, spending the night at his house was something else.

"Come on, Kelsey," Rikki moaned. "I'm not asking for anything else."

Kelsey sighed. "I don't feel comfortable invading your dad's house."

"You're there all of the time now, what's the difference?"

"I'm there during the daytime, I don't spend the night. It's not my place to."

Rikki pouted.

Kelsey rolled her eyes. "You can call me when you get up, and I'll come over to watch you open your gifts."

"Dad said it would be okay for you to spend the night in my room, I have bunk beds."

"I know, but it wouldn't feel right for me to sleep there, even in your room."

The girl's pout grew.

How can I give her that wish, but not spend the night at Neil's house? Kelsey frowned. *Perfect! Neil may not like it, but that's his problem.*

"What if you and your dad spent the night here?"

Rikki's head cocked to one side.

"Think about it," Kelsey said, "You could bunk with me while your dad slept in your room, and I wouldn't have to worry about leaving the cats overnight."

"I could talk to Dad. It was his idea to have you over."

Kelsey blinked. *I thought it was Rikki's idea, not Neil's.* "I'd feel more comfortable here, with you two and the pets."

Rikki nodded. "Can we talk to Dad when he comes over this afternoon?"

"Of course."

"Kelsey, can you help me pick out something for Dad?"

She shrugged. "I'm not sure what he'd like —"

"I know what I want to get him, I need someone to drive me to the mall."

"We'll go the first day of your holiday break."

"Perfect."

Rikki squealed in excitement as she held up the box set of DVDs on Christmas Morning. "How'd you know I love the show?" It was every single season of the revival part of a science fiction series, plus all the specials.

Neil and Kelsey exchanged a grin.

"Thank your dad, it was his idea," she said.

"Actually, your mom wanted to know what to get you and — Oomph," Neil groaned.

Rikki jumped on his lap and hugged him tightly.

"You two are the best parents ever," she exclaimed and grabbed her mother.

Kelsey's head connected hard with Neil's.

They yelped in unison.

Rikki leapt up and yelled as she ran out of the room, "I'm going to call Taffy and let her know."

Kelsey rubbed the side of her head and cringed. "Did you get a goose egg from that too?"

"That girl doesn't know her own strength." He cricked his neck and grinned. "I should have known she was going to go nuts when she saw that. She's been a fan since the series premiere."

"Next time, we'll wear helmets," Kelsey promised and

leaned her arm into his. "Something tells me we're going to be watching a lot of DVDs over the rest of the holiday break."

"That's fine."

"I've only seen a couple of episodes of it, and not any of the newer ones. I don't have a clue who she's talking about, and she's been grumbling at me."

His arm went around her shoulders. "Look at it like this, watching all of the episodes will get you in the loop."

"True."

Damn, she looks so cute when she's confused.

He quickly cut off that train of thought and gestured to the hoodie on the floor beside them. "You remembered my favourite team."

She grinned. The New York baseball team sweater was a joint gift from her, Rikki and the pets. "It's not every day you meet a Canadian who loves an American team. Most people I know are Toronto fans," she replied.

"I don't remember telling you."

"You wore their shirts a lot, so it was easy to remember."

Kelsey and her photographic memory.

He laughed and pulled something out from behind a pillow. "Merry Christmas, Kelsey."

She eyed the small, gaily wrapped box warily. "What's this?"

"Not much, it's something I thought you'd like."

I hope she loves it, and Rikki better have given me the correct size. It'll be a bitch to get it fixed or replaced if she hates it.

She gave him a puzzled glance and slowly started to peel off the wrapping. When she pulled off the cover, she gasped with wide eyes, and put a hand over her mouth.

Shit, she hates it.

"Don't you like it?"

She caressed the small silver and onyx ring with a sniffle. "I love it."

"But."

"I can't accept it."

"Why not?"

"It's not appropriate."

His eyes rolled. "How so?"

She let out a long breath. "Friends don't give friends rings."

"That's bullshit, Kelsey, and you know it. You're more than a friend to me."

She peered up at him. "Says who?"

His cheeks warmed under the scrutiny. "We're Rikki's parents and members of the same family. An unconventional one, but we're still a family."

Kelsey stared at him for a moment and started to nod slowly. "I don't think it's right for you to give me a ring."

Neil sighed. "It was Rikki's idea to get it for you, so technically it's from both of us." When she opened her mouth to protest again, he added, "Mothers are allowed to get rings from their children."

She nodded again.

Is she crying? Not yet.

He tightened his arm around her. "She's going to be disappointed if you don't wear it."

Kelsey shot him a filthy look and with a shake of her head, took the ring out of the box. "I don't want to hurt her feelings."

He grinned triumphantly.

"Put it on before she comes back."

She slid it on her right ring finger and admired it. "How did you know what size — oh, never mind. Rikki told you."

He laughed. "She picked it out and insisted on getting it in silver. She knows you like it better than gold."

"She's too smart for our good," Kelsey grumbled jokingly. She reached up to touch his cheek and rested her head on his shoulder. "Thanks."

"You're welcome," he whispered.

His gaze locked with hers and he felt something nudge

him, hard. Without thinking, he nuzzled his forehead against hers, and his eyes slid shut as he leaned toward her.

"Punky, get back here, you brat!"

Neil and Kelsey jumped and straightened as the corgi blew past them and into the kitchen with a ribbon in his mouth. Rikki skittered around the corner in her sock feet and almost slid out of the room as she tried to catch her dog.

With an uncomfortable glance and chuckle, Kelsey and Neil shifted away from each other.

She stood up when an annoyed meow echoed from the next room. "Maybe I'd better help."

"Yeah," he replied and with a sigh, got up. "Hopefully that damn chowder head will let us catch him this time."

That was too fucking close.

Next time, kiss her fast, don't hold back.

Or don't kiss her at all.

He let out a long sigh as he got up and followed Kelsey into the next room.

CHAPTER FOUR

Mid January

Kelsey and Neil were enjoying some quiet time one evening while Rikki was doing homework when Kelsey asked, "What do you want to do about her birthday this year?"

Neil thought about it for a moment. "She mentioned having a few friends overnight, but she hasn't said anything about it for a while. Why? Do you have any ideas?"

"I was thinking about having a small party at my house with cake and presents, but I wasn't sure if you had anything planned for it."

He shook his head. "I'm letting Rikki decide this year. She didn't like the games and other things Gina, Ruby and I planned for it last year, and didn't let us forget it for months."

"What if we have a sleepover, but have it at my place?" Kelsey suggested. "We can set up a movie night, and if she wants, have another party at your house with cake and other things."

Neil grinned at her. "She may go for it, since she's only had Taffy over at either place. I'll ask her when she's done her homework."

When Kelsey had first moved to the area, Rikki and Taffy had alternated between either one of her parents' homes, and the Sinclair-Jesso house. In the weeks since Christmas, she had slowly started spending more time at Ruby and Gina's. Neil wondered if his daughter had a crush on Taffy's twin brother, Timothy, because she was over there so much, and had to bite his tongue each time he thought about asking her.

Kelsey peered at him. "If you're wondering if she has a crush on Tim, she doesn't."

He stared at her. "How did you—"

"Neil, you think she's growing up too fast."

He sighed, "Kelsey—"

She shifted and put a hand on his chest. "You're worried about her. However, she is trying to find her wings, and it wouldn't hurt to give her a little freedom once in a while."

It was his turn to peer at her. "And you don't know shit about being a parent?"

She batted her lashes at him and smirked. "I've learned a lot over the last few weeks, and I remember what it was like to be fourteen." Her smile faded. "Unlike me, Rikki has two parents who care, instead of one that doesn't."

He hugged her close.

She leaned into his side. *This feels too good.*

"That wasn't your fault, Kelsey. Your mom didn't know how to love anything other than the bottle. And even though you had a rough childhood, I think you turned out fine."

"Thanks," she whispered and snuggled closer to him.

Two weeks later, Rikki's birthday weekend arrived, and Kelsey was satisfied with everything. Rikki, Taffy and the four other girls invited would be there after school and they were looking forward to a long weekend of movies, gossip and fun.

However, the instant the girls walked into the house with Punky, bedlam ensued. After the girls said hello to her and introduced themselves, they made the mistake of not locking the dog in Rikki's bedroom.

Excited to have so many admirers at once, Punky took off like a bullet the instant he was off his leash and made a lunge for the cats. Sammy and Casey hissed and zoomed off in different directions. The corgi's playful nature took over and the promise of a treat could not calm him.

The girls laughed and tried to catch him.

Kelsey slid down the wall to land on her rump and watched the scene unfold with a grimace.

Insanity seemed to follow that corgi wherever he went.

I think he creates chaos out of boredom, or because he likes it!

Finally, the girls rounded up the eager canine and managed to sweet-talk him into Rikki's room with treats and the promise of belly rubs.

Kelsey thought the worst of the craziness was over once Punky was distracted with food.

Unfortunately, she had forgotten how noisy teenage girls could be when they were not absorbed in a movie or TV show. The blare echoing out of the house was deafening, punctured by squeals and giggles, and she wondered how any parent could survive a few hours of it without going deaf or losing their mind.

She was right by the speaker for the doorbell when it rang. She ran for it with a sigh and a prayer it was someone quiet, preferably an adult with chocolate who would rescue her from the madness.

Kelsey opened the door and sagged against the wall with relief when she saw Neil. "For a minute, I thought it was the cops," she explained as she moved back to let him inside.

He glanced toward the hallway with a wry grin and cringed at the noise level coming from Rikki's room. "Better you than me."

She stuck her tongue out at him and swiped at his arm. "If you didn't want to get run over by a bunch of screaming girls, you should have stayed away. What's up?"

"I'm dropping off a few DVDs for the girls," he replied and held them up.

Kelsey noted the titles and grinned. "Do you want to give

them to her yourself? You're welcome to come in and say hello."

Please save me.

Neil groaned and held up his hands defensively. "Uh, no, that's fine. How are you holding up? Are you ready to rip out your hair yet?"

She gave him a blank look.

"It was your idea to have the party at your place," he said.

She wanted to wipe that smug smile off his face, preferably with one of his dirty socks. *Better yet, Punky's favourite blanket. That thing is disgusting.*

She grabbed a DVD case out of his hand and lightly whapped him over the head with it. "You could have warned me about the noise and insanity!"

He snickered. "Some things are best learned when you're in the middle of it."

An evil grin spread across her face as a way of revenge came to her. "Would you like a coffee?"

Neil glanced at the hallway again and raised an eyebrow at her. "Rule one of having a sleepover is that if you're a single parent, no other adults are allowed, especially if you volunteered."

Kelsey mockingly glared at him. "The next time she has a sleepover, it's at your place, and you're on your own."

His left eyelid twitched. "I was joking."

She giggled. "I knew you were yanking my chain."

"You can't blame a guy for trying."

Her smile softened. "Seriously, do you want a coffee? I'll make sure the girls don't go nuts on you if you come in."

"I can't. I have the support group this evening."

She nodded as she recalled it. It was Friday night and the group for runaway teens. Neil had switched weeks with another leader so the other man could take a family trip. "Some other time?"

Neil's grin made her toes curl in her sneakers. "Definitely."

Their gazes locked and their smiles faded as he hesitantly reached out to cup her cheek in his palm. His thumb brushed her lower lip.

Kelsey trembled when she saw the tenderness on his face. She leaned into the soft caress and shivered as she felt his breath, soft and warm, graze her lips. She nuzzled her face against his, closed her eyes and brushed her lower lip along his.

A loud bang ripped through the house. They pulled away from each other with a jump.

Giggles and squeals echoed out of the hallway.

Neil awkwardly shoved his hands into his pockets.

Kelsey took a step backwards and wrapped her arms around her stomach.

Punky tore past them with a bra dangling from his mouth, followed by Rikki, Taffy and the other four girls spending the night.

"What in the dickens is he doing now?" Kelsey called after them with a sigh.

"Punky stole Carrie's bra and we're trying to get him before he buries it in the snow!" Taffy yelled over her shoulder.

Kelsey blinked several times. With an apologetic smile at Neil, she muttered, "I'd better help them before he eats it."

Neil was trying to hold back a snicker. "Better you than me."

She gave him a filthy look, which softened when he touched her cheek.

"I'll let you get to it." He leaned forward and placed a soft kiss on her forehead. "Night, Kelsey."

"Night," she whispered as he left, and with a shrug, jumped back into the fray.

The girls were still sleeping the following morning when Neil dropped by again, on the pretence of bringing extra treats and dog chow for Punky.

In reality, he wanted to check on Kelsey, to see if she survived the noise and chaos of her first official sleepover as Rikki's mother, and to try to talk to her in private. Their last talk had ended with that almost kiss, and the feel of her lips grazing his had him lying awake the entire night, wishing they hadn't been interrupted by six excited teenagers. Even if he didn't get a chance to finish what they'd tried to start last night, he wanted to see her, to be close to her and find out if she was upset with him for trying to bridge the gap between best friends and lovers.

Kelsey immediately dragged him into the kitchen. "We can talk in here, so the girls aren't disturbed. I need coffee, and lots of it."

Neil grinned and sat on a chair after he deposited the bag of dog food and treats on the floor next to him. "Long night?"

She shot him a filthy look over her shoulder.

He laughed. "What time did everyone crash? You look worn out."

"I think Carrie went to sleep around two, and the rest weren't that long following her. Taffy and Rikki were the last to go, I think that was around five," she muttered and poured coffee into two mugs. "Punky wound up coming over with me at one point, I guess he couldn't have a nap with all of the confusion." She put a mug in front of him. "It's bad when chowder head doesn't want to be the centre of attention."

She continued to jabber about the night's events, a signal to him about how she really felt. He rose to his feet and stood behind her.

She kept her head lowered and muttered with a shake of her head, "To top it off, Punky hurled in Brenda's suitcase, and I—"

"Kelsey, you're rambling."

"I'm telling you what happened last night—"

"You always babble when something's bothering you." He touched her shoulder and prompted, "What's really on your mind?"

"Nothing," she mumbled without looking at him.

"Bullshit. Something is troubling you if you're talking faster than a race car."

She let out a long sigh and tapped a fingernail on the side of her dark blue mug. "Um, about last night."

"What about it?" He stared down at her and waited for her to continue.

"Were you going to—you know?" She glanced up at him and shifted uncomfortably.

His fingers brushed her jaw. "Was I going to what?"

"Come on, Neil, like you don't remember what happened just before the girls ran through the house?"

"I remember it." *Too well. If we hadn't been interrupted, god knows what would have happened.* His body tightened in anticipation at the memory of her sweet lips touching his.

"And what?" she asked after a moment, with her gaze glued elsewhere.

"I would have—Jesus Christ almighty!" Neil jumped backwards with a startled yelp as something touched his leg. He glared downwards at Punky, who was standing on his hind legs with his bum wagging excitedly.

Kelsey sighed. "Who let you out?"

Punky let out a sharp bark and pawed at Neil's leg.

"Shut up," Kelsey hissed. "Don't wake the girls!"

The dog dropped to all fours and his ears went back.

Neil and Kelsey exchanged a pained look and after a moment, they muttered "Chowder head," in unison and started to laugh.

Kelsey relaxed after Punky's interruption. She wasn't mad at the dog for breaking the uncomfortable air between her and Neil. However, she wasn't impressed with how Neil had seemed to pull back from her after the dog had surprised them. He'd been about to tell her something, and thanks to Punky, she might never find out.

He was still there, listening to Rikki and her friends enthusiastically give him a run-down of the previous night's adventures and what they planned to do that day.

It was a two-night event, and the thought of listening to another dance song made her nauseated. She was considering calling Gina and Ruby to come over to give her some female sanity when Rikki announced the group was heading to Taffy's house for a few minutes.

"Why are you going over there?" Neil asked.

The girls exchanged grins. "I have a new CD I wanted to share with Rikki, and I forgot it," Taffy explained, and the entire group nodded in synch.

"Taffy's thinking about Brandon too much to remember anything," Leanne giggled.

"Shut up. Rikki's dad may tell her moms," Carrie exclaimed.

"Oops." Leanne slapped her hand over her mouth.

"Are your parents' home?" Kelsey asked with a stern look at Taffy. "If they're not, none of you are going anywhere."

"I just called the house. Mom is shopping, but Mama Ruby's home. Call if you want to check." Taffy's tone carried a dare.

Heck with it. If she says Ruby's home, I'll take her word for it.

"If you're going to be more than an hour, call so we don't worry," Neil said.

The group nodded eagerly. Rikki made a grab for her dog. "We'll take Punky with us so he can have a walk and get out of the house for a bit." She snapped his leash onto his collar before he could escape and started to drag him with her.

The rest of the group tagged along, with waves and their goodbyes echoing out of the living room in their wake.

CHAPTER FIVE

Neil's initial anger at Punky for barging in on him and Kelsey abated once he saw Taffy emerge from the living room. The dog came in at the right time.

What if it was their daughter, or worse, one of her friends instead of chowder head who had seen them? He shouldn't have tried to talk to her about their almost kiss last night until he knew they were going to be alone.

He placed his mug in the sink after the girls' exit with a sly grin. They had given him the perfect opportunity to finish his talk with Kelsey about their next step.

Kelsey let out a happy sigh. "Do you hear that?" she asked.

He glanced at her. "Hear what?"

"It's so quiet. It's the first bit of peace I've heard in over eighteen hours."

"Enjoy it while it lasts, the girls will be back shortly. Unless they con Gina and Ruby into letting them hang out in Taffy's room for a few hours."

"In a way, I hope they do. Even an hour's peace would be wonderful. I love them all, but they can be so tiring." She leaned her head back and stretched her neck.

Neil's pulse quickened as his gaze was drawn to her, and it slowly followed the curve of her throat, down to the small swell of her breasts. The compulsion to talk to her about their status quo was quieted by a more primitive, urgent call as his focus moved upwards and landed on her mouth.

Two steps closed the distance between them, and it turned into a primal scream of need and longing as he leaned

44

forward to crush her lips under his.

Her body tensed and she didn't move.

Oh, shit. Did I read her wrong last night? I thought she wanted me to kiss her.

He was about to pull back when he felt her hands reach up to fist around the front of his shirt and she leaned into him. He relaxed and scraped his bottom lip along hers. She shivered and parted her lips, allowing him access. He deepened the kiss and shuddered as he tasted her fully for the first time.

The feel of her lean body pressing into his, the soft smell of her skin, and the musky taste of her on his tongue drove his longing to be with her to an all-time high. His fingers tangled in her hair as he lost himself in everything about her.

When Neil kissed her, Kelsey thought she was dreaming again. She reached up to slap herself awake, and froze as her hand connected with a warm, firm body that wasn't her own. It took her a few seconds to realize it was real and Neil was kissing her. She shivered at the gentle warmth of his mouth on hers and let her feelings for him rise to the surface.

If this was going to be the only time he kissed her, she was going to enjoy it. She slid her arms around his waist, thrust her tongue into his mouth and clung to him as their mouths moved in synch and desire started to rise.

She almost lost it when he pulled back and rested his forehead against hers.

She snuggled closer to him and sighed softly.

"Kelsey, I'm—" he whispered after a moment and his mouth caressed hers again.

"If you're going to apologize, I'll shoot you," she threatened softly.

His teeth grazed her jaw, and she felt him continue nipping and kissing his way downwards. "No freaking way," he murmured as his lips brushed the hollow of her throat. "I was going to say I wish I had done that sooner."

Kelsey trembled, and her head fell backwards. She let out a long, loud whimper when his hand moved from her neck to her hip and he pulled her hard against his aroused member. "Huh?"

It was tough to think when he was doing that.

"Christmas," he groaned. "It almost happened that morning, and it's been too damn crazy with Rikki being around, else I would have kissed you before today."

Kelsey recalled their almost kiss on that day. She had been disappointed it hadn't happened and wondered if he would ever go through with it. When Neil started pulling back from her after that, she'd let it go and thought she had dreamed it.

She leaned her head into his and raked her nails down his back as she murmured, "I thought it was a passing thing and you were caught up in Rikki's excitement."

Neil lifted his head so he could stare deep into her eyes. "I wouldn't have tried it then or last night if I didn't want to do it."

She nodded and pressed closer to him. One question remained. "Is it because I'm Rikki's mom, or—"

She was cut off by Neil's mouth crushing hers again. Kelsey leaned into it, the rest of her words forgotten as her fantasies about him became reality again. Tongues warred for several minutes as she gave in to her feelings and desire for the amazing man who was kissing her.

Sanity slapped them upside of the head when a car backfired outside.

Neil pulled back and gruffly panted between harsh, hungry kisses, "We should stop. The girls could be back at any second."

Kelsey had forgotten about Rikki and her friends. "Good point."

His mouth swiftly covered hers again in a long promise

and demand of surrender. "I wish the girls would stay at Taffy's, because I want you to—" A groan escaped his throat, and he crushed her to him.

"Do you think we have the time to talk about this now, or should we wait?"

Neil let out a long breath and rested his cheek on top of her head. "I'd like to talk about it now, so I'm not going crazy wondering what you're thinking. Tell me what you want, sweetheart."

She closed her eyes and whispered, "Neil, I want—"

A slamming door and the distinctive sound of dog claws on tile echoed through the house. Kelsey froze and stared up at Neil as an excited bark preceded Punky zooming into the kitchen.

"Kelsey? Dad? We're back!" Rikki yelled from the entryway.

With a sad smile, Kelsey quickly pulled out of Neil's arms.

"We'll finish this later," Neil whispered before he turned away from Kelsey.

Kelsey stared at his back, shock reverberating through her body.

Did he just kiss me?

He glanced over his shoulder and winked.

Holy shit. He did.

She bit her lip and hoped it wasn't a one-time thing.

After Neil left, doubts started flooding Kelsey's mind when she remembered he hadn't answered her question if his attraction to her was because she was Rikki's biological mother or not. Their talk about their feelings for each other couldn't come soon enough, and Kelsey wanted it over with so they could move forward somehow. She knew things would not be the same even if they decided to go back to being only friends, and there would be a distance between them.

The doubts kept screaming at her even through the

confusion of having a house filled with teenagers, two cats almost climbing the curtains in their play, and a corgi running from room to room in his excitement.

The night hours passed slowly as the cats and Punky slept curled up next to her, and her misgivings about Neil went in a continuous loop through her brain. She started to analyze every nuance, gesture and word they'd exchanged over the course of the day and in the weeks since she had moved home to Nova Scotia, and in the years before that.

With a long sigh, she started thinking back to when she had first met him, and the time before she had left the area.

He became her best friend in the months after her short stay at the shelter, before she left the province to find work. They spent hours together almost every day, talking about anything that interested them and making plans for the future.

Neil wanted to go back to school, get his master's in social work and continue working with children in the system. Having grown up in various foster homes, he knew how tough it was for a foster child to have any stability, and sometimes all a youth needed was someone who believed in them, like he hoped to be.

Kelsey had told him things that no one else knew. From how her mother drank since she was a toddler, her father's affair that eventually saw him leaving her mother when she was twelve, the beatings that were a part of her everyday life since she was a child, and her vow to never have any children.

It was part of the reason why she had given Rikki up for adoption over a decade ago. It had been the right choice, despite her love for the little girl she had borne.

Although Neil understood, he tried to convince her not to shun motherhood. She was kind to the younger residents of the shelter and made several friends and admirers in the three months she lived there. She refused to listen to his advice and considered getting her tubes tied so she wouldn't have to give up another child or have an abortion.

His words must have stuck somewhere in the back of her mind, because she decided to go on the pill instead, and if she was dating someone, insisted they use a condom to be extra cautious. The idea of having a child still terrified her, but it lessened a little when her feelings for Neil started to grow beyond friendship and she started dreaming of a lifetime with him.

Her fantasies of the future were shattered a year after they met, when the rumors of him dating a woman who was closer to his age and not on the fringes of society hit her ears.

After she met Rita Hunter, Kelsey believed she could never be Neil's ideal mate. Rita was beautiful, sophisticated, intelligent, and friendly, someone who complimented him in every aspect.

Unlike Kelsey, Rita was the definition of stability.

Kelsey moved to Ontario two weeks later, to find work and finish her education. She kept her promise to Neil and others she met to keep in touch, although updates on her progress were sporadic. He and Rita were married less than a year after her move.

Her last communication with Neil before he had come to her with the news about Rikki had been four years ago, a month after she moved to Montreal, and five years after his marriage to Rita.

She hadn't known he was widowed, or of the chance Rita's daughter was her biological child, until he emailed her with the news he and Rikki were going to be in the area, and their conversation at her apartment.

Knowing Rikki was her biological daughter had been a shock. Rikki looked enough like her adoptive mother and stepfather to be their child, not someone else's.

Thoughts of Rikki's looks brought a picture of her real father to Kelsey's mind, and she smiled sadly when she remembered her ex-boyfriend's reluctant understanding of her decision to give up their daughter for adoption.

If he hadn't gotten in with the wrong people, I would have let him and his family have her. He was a decent guy, and in a lot of ways I wish he was still around to meet her.

With a soft sniffle, Kelsey rolled onto her side to bury her face into her pillow and cried herself to sleep.

Late the following afternoon, Kelsey dropped Taffy off at her house, and after taking a deep breath to alleviate some of her nervousness, drove Rikki and Punky to Neil's.

She felt unsure how to act around him, despite the promised discussion and the sly looks they shared yesterday.

What if it was just a passing thing?

Kelsey knew she couldn't maintain an indifferent attitude about it, now that she knew what it was like to feel his mouth on hers, and her feelings for him returned and magnified.

She didn't want to run again.

Neil's smile was bright when he opened the door. As Rikki and the dog blew past him after a "Hi, Dad!" from their daughter and a bark from Punky in greeting, his gaze met hers and softened.

"Hey," he whispered before he gave her a hug.

Kelsey's doubts started to fade, and she started to relax when she felt the lean, warm strength of his body. "Hi."

More of her remaining anxiety left as his mouth brushed hers.

Maybe it's not a passing thing after all. She leaned into him and elation started to rise as he deepened the kiss.

Disappointment surged through her when he pulled back. "Best if Rikki doesn't see it yet," he murmured.

She understood. "Later?"

"Later," he replied, and he put a little more distance between them.

Kelsey stayed while Rikki gave her father a confusing run-down on the weekend's activities. She sat on the couch beside Neil, with her arm brushing his from time to time. Rikki sprawled on the floor in front of them with Punky on his back beside her.

"Rikki, go get your stuff ready for school," Neil prompted after an hour.

"Why?"

"I want to talk to your mom for a few minutes."

"Yeah, and I bet it's about me. You always do that when you want to talk about something I did, so I don't hear it," she muttered. "I didn't do a damn thing this time."

The teenager moved her gaze to her mother.

Kelsey held up a hand. "Do what your father tells you."

As Rikki's fading footsteps turned into the slam of her bedroom door, Kelsey turned her head to meet Neil's gaze.

His lips were in a firm line. "She'd kill us if she knew she's not the centre of attention this time."

Kelsey's laughter was cut off when Neil's fingers cupped the back of her head and his mouth crushed hers. She sighed into his mouth and cuddled closer to his side as desire and love started to rise in her body and mind.

She felt his warm breath against her lips as he whispered, "It's not because you're her mother, Kelsey, there's more to it than that."

Her eyes opened. "What do you mean?"

His mouth brushed hers again. "It would have happened even if she wasn't ours. You were always special to me."

Something tickled at the back of Kelsey's mind, which disappeared when he kissed her again. Her hand moved from her lap to his leg, and she started to massage the muscles hidden under the denim.

"Save it for later, I don't want to have a hard-on when Rikki could walk in any moment." He kissed her hard again and pulled back. "Best if we stop, else she's going to get an early education or get grossed out."

Although Kelsey was disappointed, she nodded in under-standing and rested her head on his shoulder. Elation surged through her as his arm tightened around her shoulders and he kissed the top of her head.

Chapter Six

As soon as the school bus disappeared around the corner Wednesday morning, Neil quickly rounded up Punky and secured him in his fenced in area, which was located just off the garage. The dog could run around without hindrance, had plenty of food and water, and was able to get into the downstairs mud room, where he could nap on an old sofa or play with toys.

Anticipation fueled Neil's steps, and he was at Kelsey's front door a few minutes after he left his driveway.

"You're here awfully early. Is there something wrong with Rikki?" she asked after she let him inside.

He shook his head and pulled her into his arms. "Nothing's wrong. I couldn't wait to see you without worrying about Rikki seeing us."

She smiled, slid her arms around his neck, and nestled her body against his. "I'll forgive you. Do you want a coffee? I just made a pot."

"It can wait a few minutes," he whispered and brushed his mouth along hers.

Kelsey responded with a shiver of delight and snuggled closer to him. "Mm."

After they settled on the couch with Kelsey snuggled up to Neil's side, he let out a long breath. "Kelsey, I've been thinking about things, and —" What he wanted to say evaporated, forgotten as a little uneasiness penetrated the room.

She stared at him warily. He felt her starting to stiffen.

Aw, shit. Why did I start off like that? She closes the door and

53

welds it shut when someone rejects her. No second chances.

It had taken her a long time to open up and trust him years ago, and only after he had proved he'd never hurt her, mentally or physically. He hoped he never tested her faith in him, because he didn't want to lose her.

He leaned forward and placed a long, hard kiss on her mouth in reassurance. "I'm here for the long run. I wouldn't have kissed you if I was going to drop you the next day."

"Sorry." She kissed him softly, and relaxed.

Neil pulled her head down to his shoulder and rested his jaw on her forehead. Her hand slid up his chest and she nuzzled her face against his neck. "Come on, Kelsey, spill it."

"This isn't a fling for me either. I want to see where this takes us."

He closed his eyes in relief. "We have lots of time to figure that out."

"I wonder what will happen if it doesn't work out. I'm scared something's going to ruin it, and it'll hurt me to see you after—"

He silenced her by putting his thumb across her lips. "If you're not going to fight to make this work, you're setting us up for failure." Tenderly, he stroked her lips with his fingers and hugged her closer to his side. "It takes both people to make a go of it."

She lifted her head to stare at him with tears in her eyes. "I care about you, Neil, so much that the thought of not having you in my life makes me sick."

"Then never give up on me."

"I won't, as long as you don't give up on me."

He kissed her again. "Never."

"Are we going to sleep together?"

"That's going to happen at some point, although we'd better keep that quiet for a while." He smiled, and smugness settled in his gut.

Their eyes met, and in unison, they said, "Rikki."

"You're the expert, so tell me what you think is best for her," she said and fingered his shirt collar.

"On one hand, I know she wants you in her life full time, more so than you are now, but—"

"You're scared she's going to be pissed off you're dating again."

"Yes, or she'll start dreaming of having a brother or sister. She hates being an only child."

"Maybe we could start testing the waters with hints when we think the time is right," Kelsey suggested and frowned. "That's if she doesn't figure it out on her own."

"Either way, we're going to get an earful."

"Do you want to start things now?"

"It can wait." His lips grazed her cheek.

"When?"

"I don't know. I don't want any chance of Rikki catching us yet, so it may not happen for a while." His mouth met hers, and his free hand started caressing her ribs, just below her breast. "Dammit, you feel so good though."

"She is in school."

He shuddered as her fingers touched the inner part of his leg. With a low groan, he firmly moved her hand up to his chest. "I want to, so bad I can taste it, but I'm falling behind as it is. I'm on a deadline."

She sighed softly and her head flopped down on his shoulder. "I forgot about that."

He grinned and tipped her chin up with his thumb so he could kiss her. "I can take breaks during work hours, you know."

"Another time, huh?"

His mouth brushed hers again. "Yeah. When it happens, I'm going to want it to last the whole night. We're going to take our time."

Kelsey sighed as Neil's lips covered hers fully, then started to tremble when he thrust his tongue deep into her mouth.

When he finally lifted his head, they were gasping for breath and shaking from barely restrained hunger.

"You should get going," she murmured.

"I don't want to, not yet." His lips brushed hers. "A few more minutes."

He felt her hand move from his neck to his belt and slide downwards.

His teeth ground together and his hips reared upwards as her fingers touched the top of his fly. "Jesus, Kelsey. I'm not going to get any work done if you keep this up."

"If you stay much longer, I'm not going to be responsible for my actions," she shot back between harsh kisses, and trailed the tip of her finger along the hard ridge of his arousal.

He shuddered violently at her touch and swallowed hard with a reluctant nod. *She touches me, and I'm fit to explode.* "Yeah, it's definitely time to go."

When he stood up, the bulge at the front of his jeans was at her eye level, and she stared at it boldly with an arrogant grin.

"Move your damn eyes. I can't calm down with you looking at me like that."

She took her time moving her gaze upwards to meet his.

He grinned sheepishly, a little embarrassed of his obvious reaction to her, and held out a hand.

Kelsey took it and rose to her feet. She slid her arms around his waist and sighed. "That was a little fast. I'll be easy on you next time."

He snickered and rested his jaw on her temple. "If I didn't have that damn deadline hanging over my head, we wouldn't have stopped. Too bad you're working the closing shift this weekend — Rikki plans on being at Taffy's both nights."

"I'd switch with Enid, but it's my turn to do the crappy shift."

"You're still going to stop in on your way to work, right?"

He didn't want a day to go by that he didn't see her.

"If I'm running late, I'll talk to you on the phone instead," she promised and lifted her head to stare up at him. "I will be over later this evening. Rikki wants to borrow a sweater for the dance and asked me to bring one over."

"Dammit, I'm chaperoning."

"I remember."

"I could back out."

Kelsey shook her head. "Go. I have to get to bed early, I work in the morning."

"I'll call you during the dance."

"I'd love that." She leaned over and gave him a long, lingering kiss.

The weekend passed without Kelsey and Neil sneaking in any private time.

Rikki and Taffy wound up spending the weekend at Neil's house after Taffy's twin brother, Tim had to be taken to the emergency room for the third time in two months.

The entire time she was there, Kelsey exchanged pained glances with Neil and silently raged along with the girls. Her plans to have a few stolen moments with him were trashed. Kelsey wished Ruby and Gina would duct tape Tim to the ceiling, so he couldn't pull off any more stunts.

Monday rolled around, and although Kelsey had the day off, crunch time was upon Neil. He had three days to get his latest article finished and sent to his publisher. Between the craziness of having the girls at the house unexpectedly and other things invading his work time, he had to knuckle down and work on it all day without taking any more than a few minutes away from it.

Kelsey stayed away during his work time, so she wouldn't distract him. She contented herself with talking to him on the phone or seeing him after Rikki was home from school on her days off. They managed to steal a few moments along the way, just long enough for a quick kiss or a gentle caress when Rikki wasn't in the room.

Tuesday, she found her old writing notebook at the bottom of a box and was about to put it back when something tingled at the back of her mind. She caressed the leather-bound book, a nineteenth birthday gift from Neil, and with a shrug, set the journal aside and put the box away.

She saw it on her nightstand later that night, and without thinking, flipped to a clean page and started writing. Only ideas were coming to her, and her pencil flew across the page as she wrote them down.

When she was finished, she had filled over ten pages, and only two hours had passed.

Wednesday, more ideas came to her, and she filled another five pages.

She set it aside, and as she lay down to rest, she wondered if that was just a flash in the pan or she was able to write again. She glanced at it, and a slow smile formed across her face.

Thursday, Kelsey found Rikki and Punky on her doorstep after work. She opened the house and they zoomed in.

Rikki flopped down at the square kitchen table and grumbled, "Dad's working again."

"I thought he was done with that article and sent it off yesterday," Kelsey commented and placed a glass of juice in front of her daughter.

"He did. I guess they offered him a little extra if he did another short one for them. It's due Saturday, I think," Rikki muttered with a pout.

Disappointment rose in Kelsey's chest and she turned away so her daughter wouldn't see the sadness on her face. If Neil had another deadline ahead of him, she didn't want to invade on his work time, and that meant any alone time was out of the question.

It seemed each time they thought they might have some time together, something came along and messed it up, like work or kids. At this rate, they might get around to having sex by the end of the decade.

She yanked out the elastic holding her hair back and shoved it into her pocket so she wouldn't slam her fist onto the cupboard in anger. *Hold it together, girl.*

"Kelsey?" Rikki touched her arm.

She jumped. "What?"

"I asked you three times if you were working tomorrow."

"I have the day off. Why?"

Rikki sat down again. "If Dad isn't done, may I spend the night here so I don't bother him?"

"As long as you do your homework before you get on the phone with Taffy."

"Aw, Kelsey."

She held up a hand. "You know the rules, Rikki. What goes at your dad's place goes here too."

The teenager rolled her eyes. "I'll do my damn home-work." she muttered.

Kelsey rubbed her temples. The combination of the frustration of raising a teenager, working odd hours, and not spending time with Neil was giving her a headache. "Cut the swearing, Erika Lynn, or you're going to lose your phone again."

Rikki growled and glared at her. "You and Dad say it all of the time, so why can't I?"

The backtalk was too much. She pointed to the hallway and snapped, "Erika Lynn, homework, now!"

When Rikki didn't move, Kelsey snarled, "March."

The girl instantly hopped to her feet and ran out of the room, with Punky on her heels.

Kelsey picked up the dishcloth and threw it at the fridge to let out some of her aggravation.

"Fucking asshole! Mother fucker! Fuck, fuck, fuck, fuck, fuck!"

She kicked the cupboard as a final release.

When the surge of anger faded, guilt flooded her. She shouldn't have taken her irritation out on Rikki. It wasn't her fault that Neil took on another job that required him to work round the clock so he could provide a good home for their daughter.

With a long sigh and tears burning her throat, she walked down the hall to Rikki's room and knocked on the door.

"I'm doing my homework."

"I'm sorry," Kelsey said.

Silence echoed back at her.

"Rikki, I've had a long day. Work was crazy, I had a lot of rude customers, and I'm really tired and pissed off about a few things. You came over here to spend some time with me, and to give your dad some quiet time. I shouldn't have taken it all out on you." She wiped her eyes with her sleeve and waited.

The door opened after a minute and her daughter stared up at her with a sheepish grin.

Kelsey grabbed Rikki in a bear hug and wouldn't let go of her.

"I'm sorry too," the girl said after a moment. "I shouldn't have cursed at you or bitched about homework right after you got home."

Kelsey pulled back to frame Rikki's face in her hands and smiled. "I think we need a little time to relax and forget our troubles. How does some chocolate ice cream and a marathon of your favourite TV show sound?"

Rikki beamed. "I'll finish my homework now, so we can get to it."

"Call your dad and tell him you're spending the night here.

After that, get your pajamas on. This is going to be a girl's night, no boys or problems allowed." Kelsey said and nuzzled her face against Rikki's with a grin.

"Dad just texted me!" Rikki's excited yell echoed out of the bathroom the next morning while she was getting ready for school.

Kelsey dropped the jeans she was pulling out of the bureau and winced at her daughter's bellow. "Inside voice." She scooped the fallen denim off the floor and shook her head.

Rikki poked her head into the room via the bathroom entryway. She was grinning. "He's almost done with the article and says if he has it done before this afternoon, the three of us can do something fun tomorrow."

A glimmer of hope shimmered up Kelsey's spine. If he finished things that morning, there was a chance of having a little time alone with him before Rikki came home from school.

She turned her head and started digging through her t-shirts so Rikki wouldn't see the goofy expression on her face. "Yeah, sure," she said airily and tried to keep her voice level.

"Awesome," Rikki squealed and ran back into the bathroom.

Three hours later, Neil rolled his neck to alleviate some of the stiffness in it. He had stayed up most of the night, working on getting the second article for the magazine out of the way, and finally finished its final edit a moment earlier. His eyes burned, his hands were numb, his entire body ached, and he was looking forward to sleeping the entire afternoon without worrying about a deadline hanging over his head.

He uploaded it into an email attachment and was typing up a quick outline of it for the editor when the doorbell rang. He ignored it and kept typing.

When it echoed through the house a second time a few minutes later, he rolled his eyes and let out a curse.

He stomped out to the front door and opened it with a bark of "What?" and jumped when a tri-colored streak blew past him with a happy whine.

He whipped his head around to see a corgi bottom making a beeline for the hallway. "Punky? What are you doing here? I thought you were at Kelsey's."

"He was, and I thought I'd bring him home a little early. I'll go home if you're going to growl at me."

Neil winced as Kelsey's voice broke through the fog in his brain. He glanced up at the ceiling and sighed. "Kelsey, wait!"

He strode out the door and caught up to her just as she hit the bottom stair. He gently grabbed her arm and tugged her backwards. "Sorry," he mumbled as he led her into the house.

Kelsey shrugged. "I should have called to check if you were done yet."

He shut the door and motioned for her to take off her jacket. "I was about to hit send when you arrived. Go get a coffee. I'll only be a few minutes." He kissed her quickly in reassurance and strode off.

Kelsey walked into the room with two mugs in her hands. "Are you done?"

"Yes, I just sent it off." Neil took the offered mug with a sigh.

Although Kelsey had walked past his office before, she had never been inside it. She noted that unlike the rest of the house, bedlam ruled. Stacks of files and papers titled precariously on one corner of the desk, papers were strewn about, and file storage boxes were stacked in an unorganized manner. Neil was meticulous about order, which drove her and Rikki crazy sometimes. Seeing disarray in his workspace made him seem a little more normal to Kelsey.

"Have you slept at all?" she asked as she noticed the weariness on his face and the black circles under his eyes.

"Not since—what day is it?" He rolled his shoulders and closed his eyes.

"It's Friday."

He nodded. "I think I caught a couple of hours yesterday. Or was that Wednesday? Don't start, Kelsey. I'll crash later."

She shrugged and set her mug on the desk. "Rikki and Punky can stay with me again tonight, that way you can sleep without worrying about them. I'll drop them off on my way to work tomorrow."

It would give him almost a full day to recover and give her some extra time with their daughter. Kelsey knew it wouldn't be a problem for the teenager once she heard how exhausted her dad was. Rikki worried about Neil a lot when he was on a long work bender.

He sighed wearily. "You don't have to do that. I've done it on less sleep, and I'll do it again."

She peered down at him. "Do I have to remind you that part of the reason why I moved down here was to help you? You're always looking out for me when I'm ready to drop. Let me return the favour."

He nodded reluctantly after a moment. "You win."

She grinned triumphantly, and her smile faded when he rubbed the heel of his hand over his forehead. When she touched his arm, she felt the stiffness in his body from being hunched over the keyboard for hours, and she could see the fatigue in his movements.

She moved behind him and started rubbing his neck and shoulders to soothe his tension.

Neil let out a long groan.

She could feel his stress oozing out of his body and she smiled when she saw his eyes close.

He leaned backwards to rest his head against her chest with a long sigh.

"How long of a stretch was it this time?" She rubbed circles over his shoulder blades.

He let out a pleased sound. "Not sure, maybe ten or twelve hours."

"You have to take breaks once in a while, or else you're going to get sick." She moved a hand to his face and ran the back of her fingers along the stubble of his cheek to emphasize her point.

He grabbed her hand and held it still. "I can't pay the bills unless I do this once in a while."

"But—"

"Kelsey, stop it." He turned his head and opened his eyes to meet her gaze. His free hand lifted to touch her jaw. "It's no big deal. I'll be fine, once I crash for a few hours and have a shower. Stop worrying."

"No big deal? You're almost falling asleep at the keyboard and—"

He swiveled the chair to face her and slapped a hand over her mouth. "I told you to be quiet."

She stared down at him with narrowed eyes and pushed his hand away. "Promise me you won't do this again."

"I can't do that."

She narrowed her eyes at him. "Bullshit."

"Sometimes the editor at this magazine will demand more or change things completely at the last minute. It's either go on a bender when it happens or miss the deadline. If I want to get paid, I have to do it."

He stroked her cheek. "A lot of the time, I can get it in long before the due date. This one doesn't understand that screaming for something totally different really messes things up for the writer. We have to redo everything from the research to the piece itself. She decided to throw a few extras at me without warning. If I want to keep working for her, I have to go without sleep for a couple of days. Understand?"

She shrugged. "How often does this happen?"

"It's happened to me once or twice in the last year." He gave her a lopsided smile and ran his thumb along her cheekbone. "Give me a day or so to recover, and you won't know I spent the last four days working on five hours' sleep."

"From now on, tell me when you do something like this. I was missing you a lot, and hearing it from Rikki made me so mad I could have choked you."

He nodded. Kelsey saw fatigue in his movements.

"Forgive me?" he asked.

"Always," she whispered and leaned forward to kiss him.

His hand slid around her neck and his free arm latched around her waist as he tugged her downwards. Her legs parted to straddle his, with her toes grazing the floor and her knees pressing against his hips. She slid her arms around his neck and sighed into his mouth as the tension from the argument left the room.

This was what she'd wanted all week, to be with him without anyone or anything else intruding.

He may be tired, but he feels so damn good.

He pulled back after a moment and nuzzled his face against her neck with a sigh. "God, I missed you," he whispered and nipped the skin at the hollow of her throat.

Kelsey shivered in pleasure and raked her fingers through his hair. "The last few days felt like a year."

"We'll make up for it," he replied, and his hand slid from her waist to her ribcage, "starting now." He kissed the side of her neck and his fingers brushed the underside of her breast.

Her gasp turned into a whimper of need when his thumb circled her nipple and he thrust his hips upward. The rigid length of him pressed against her mound and shivers of pleasure rippled through her body. She ground her body downward, and when he inhaled sharply, she raked her nails down his bicep.

He lifted his head to rest his forehead against hers, and their eyes met as longing crackled between them.

Kelsey didn't break eye contact as her hands moved to his shirt buttons and started unfastening them. Her fingers slid between the cotton and his skin, which she noted was hairless and starting to dampen with sweat.

His eyes slid closed for a moment and his breathing started to quicken as she explored the muscles of his shoulders, chest and abdomen. Not a single ounce of spare flesh was on his frame, his stomach was flat, and when she shifted in an effort to give him a little extra pleasure, she realized other places were competing for the hardest spot on his body. His cock felt like granite against her mound when she wriggled her hips closer to him.

He groaned loudly and his teeth clenched together.

Neil pushed her hands upwards to his shoulders, and he kissed her. "Easy, Kelsey," he ground out. "If you keep doing that, I'll finish in my pants. I'd rather be inside of you when that happens." He kissed her jaw and her neck as his hands covered her braless breasts.

She cried out as his thumbs circled nipples hardened by need. Her fingernails dug furrows into his skin and he shuddered beneath her when she pushed her hips downward.

One of his hands moved down her buttocks, lifting her higher, and the other one pushed her blouse upwards. His fingers slid around to her front, down her stomach and between her legs. The soft pressure of his fingers through her jeans made her shiver and mew softly in pleasure.

"God, you're so hot, Kelsey," he murmured, "I bet you're ready for me."

His fingers caressed her most intimate spot through her pants just as he took a nipple into his mouth and sucked hard.

Tingles of pleasure turned to a primitive, white-hot need to be possessed by him, but her body couldn't wait. Kelsey's head fell backwards, her back arched, and her entire body went tense as she came with a muffled shriek.

She tried wriggling away at the peak of her pleasure, but he wouldn't let go of her. His tongue circled her nipple and his fingers pressed against her once more, harder this time. Her second orgasm was longer and more intense than the first, and she couldn't contain her cries.

He lifted his head and kissed her. She panted against his lips, and as her aftershocks sent tremors through her body, she noted he was sweaty and shaking. She shifted on his lap, and he winced as his eyes squeezed shut and he pushed her away, so only the bottom of her legs touched the top of his thighs.

"Neil, what's wrong?"

He shifted uncomfortably and his head fell to her shoulder. "I think you'd better get off my lap."

"You didn't—"

"No, but I will if you don't move."

Her fingers moved to his belt buckle to start tugging on the leather. "Then let me—"

Strong hands pushed hers away. "Don't."

She determinedly moved a hand to his fly and started tugging the zipper down. "You made me come, so it's only fair."

His body convulsed, his head lifted from her shoulder, and his eyes burned into hers. His hands grabbed her wrists and firmly moved them away from him. He rested his forehead against hers and panted, "You can return the favour some other time."

"Why not now? It won't take much more to make you finish. I can give you a blow job."

Neil ground his teeth together and shook his head. "I don't want to go off in your mouth the first time I come with you."

She grinned and kissed him softly. "We can do that now."

"Rikki will be home from school soon. It's not a great idea unless you want her walking in on us while we're going at it." He patted her knee and she took the cue.

Kelsey rose to her feet and glanced at him with concern. "Are you sure?"

He stood up shakily with a nod. "I'll live."

"You're not going to masturbate, are you?"

"Will you be pissed off if I do?"

"Probably, because I'd rather make you come myself."

He let out a long, pained groan. "Kelsey, if you don't shut up, I'll-"

"Gag me and tie me up? Sounds like fun." She waggled her eyebrows suggestively.

"Go home. Now."

CHAPTER SEVEN

Taffy joined Kelsey and Rikki for the night. Their constant chatter and efforts to keep an excited corgi and two hyper cats from wrecking the house and backyard were a welcome distraction from her thoughts and kept her from recalling her actions during the stolen hour with Neil. She leapt into the chaos, laughed at the animals' antics, and listened to the girls gossip about their day.

At ten o'clock, the phone rang. Kelsey glanced at the caller ID, saw the number, grabbed the cordless phone and ran into her room for a little privacy.

"Did you get any sleep?" she asked in greeting.

Neil's chuckle echoed in her ear. "Yeah, I did, and hi to you too."

She snickered. "How long were you out?"

"I think it was eight hours. I felt almost human again by the time I woke up." He paused for a moment. "Did Rikki make it over to your house safely?"

"She's fine, Taffy's here with us for the night."

"I imagine you're up to your eyeballs in nail polish, hair stuff and girl talk." He gagged a little. "Better you than me."

"Well, if you really miss it that much, you could come over and join us."

"No thank you."

"You're welcome anytime."

"I'd rather drag you off to bed and finish what we started today."

Kelsey shivered and inhaled sharply at the husky promise

in his voice. "If I was alone right now, you'd be here and I'd be all over you," she whispered.

"Oh, yeah? Tell me," he dared.

She grinned evilly. "Well, you wouldn't be wearing anything, so I could watch you get hard and stroke yourself as I did a striptease before I gave you a blow —"

His loud groan cut her off. "Kelsey, stop. I'm on the verge of going off just picturing it."

"You asked," she replied, unable to keep the giggle out of her voice.

"Me and my big mouth. I still want you to hold on to that thought for when we're alone."

"Oh, I will," she promised.

He let out a long breath. "Maybe I'd better talk to Rikki for a few minutes, just to calm down. Talking to you makes me want to fuck you silly."

"I know, and right back at you. You can get your payback later."

"Definitely," he muttered.

Even though she and the girls had stayed up past midnight to watch a movie, Kelsey wasn't sleepy when she went to bed.

Her mind started to wander, and she finally allowed the memories from the afternoon to rise. A goofy, satisfied grin spread across her face in the darkened room as she went over everything, from her reaction to his touch, to how close they had been to fully giving in to their hunger for each other.

The fact he'd refused her offer of helping him made her sigh despite her happiness. It wasn't fair that he didn't get relief from his desire for her after he had made her come twice. Part of her wished she hadn't offered to take both girls for the night, because if they were at Taffy's house, she would sneak over to Neil's and seduce him. It wouldn't take much, considering how close he had been to taking her that day.

She grinned evilly as the thought about showing up at his door wearing nothing but a long coat popped into her mind, then decided to use it sometime when the girls were not around and both had a full night off.

Better make it a weekend, that way we have lots of time to enjoy each other.

I hope we can get a night or two together soon, because I'm going to lose it if we don't!

With a low curse to herself, Kelsey flipped onto her stomach, pulled the covers up over her head and forced herself to go to sleep.

Neil was frustrated.

He had been trying to get back to sleep after his phone call with Kelsey and had spent the last two hours trying to calm down his eager body so he could rest.

He rolled over and punched the pillow, which caused the sheet to scrape across his erect manhood. His teeth ground together as he attempted to ignore the agonizing pleasure shooting up its length, then threw the covers off in frustration.

He shouldn't have let things go that far with Kelsey yet. If he had just held her and kissed her instead of making her orgasm and pushing himself to the limit, he wouldn't be in this predicament now.

His instinct to keep a little distance between them when they were around others had been sound, because it seemed like the instant they were alone, he lost himself in her and the feelings she provoked in him. If he hadn't been so damn tired and they would have had more time before school was out for the day–

He shoved the thought away as he rolled over onto his back and glanced down at his cock in disgust. It was granite hard and standing straight up in a silent demand, and he knew only Kelsey could help him.

A brief flash of relieving it himself popped into his mind and he nixed the idea. He was forty-four years old and could wait a few more days. He had kept his sexual needs contained for over a year, so he could tolerate it for a little longer. All he needed to do was something to keep his mind from wandering and remembering Kelsey's reaction to him, and her cries of pleasure as orgasms rippled through her.

He cursed softly and tried to think of things that would calm him down. Nothing would, and he was suddenly grateful he was alone that night. If Rikki knew he was awake, she might try to talk to him, and his current mood didn't allow for arguing about her homework or whether or not she was allowed to go somewhere.

Remembering where his daughter was made his thoughts turn back to Kelsey, and he squeezed his eyes shut as another, stronger urge to bury himself inside of her somehow and come flooded his body.

With a louder curse, he leapt out of bed and went downstairs to run on the treadmill. Working himself into another state of exhaustion, this time physically, seemed to be his only option until he had Kelsey in his bed, writhing with pleasure beneath him as he plunged into her again and again until they exploded.

By the time he returned to his room and had a quick shower to wash the sweat from his body, another hour had passed. It was after one o'clock, and after he was comfortable, slumber easily claimed him.

"Dad, where are my black jeans?" Rikki's demand echoed out of her room early Tuesday morning.

Neil jumped in his desk chair at her bellow. "I don't know. Did you check the dryer?"

He turned back to the open document on the computer, his latest article for the same company he'd submitted the two pieces to last week. It was a shorter commentary, and it was due before noon on Friday. He wanted it done and sent off by Thursday afternoon at the latest, so he wouldn't have to do another bender like he had with the last ones.

"Yes, and they're not there."

"What about your bureau?"

"They're not there either."

He rolled his eyes. "Your closet?"

"Nope."

"Wear something else."

"I can't wear my phone box shirt with blue jeans, the shirt is black, and it would look weird."

He sighed and cricked his neck as he thought about where the pants in question may be hiding. "Did you leave them at your mom's place?"

"I don't know."

"Call and ask her."

"I can't, she's working days this week."

Neil's frustration started to bubble at the reminder that he wouldn't get any alone time with Kelsey until the weekend, and that wasn't a guarantee. The girls could be underfoot or her schedule could change in the blink of an eye. He hadn't seen her since Sunday evening, and barely had enough time to kiss her without the girls watching.

He tried to control his temper and muttered a few curse words under his breath as he saved the document, just in case Rikki missed the bus and needed a ride to school. "Then pick out something else to wear."

"I can't, I promised Brenda we'd dress up like twins to-day."

His eyes rolled skyward in a silent plea to help him keep his cool. Being a single dad hadn't been easy even when Rikki was eleven and didn't care about makeup or being a part of the popular crowd. Things were more difficult now that she was a teenager, on the cusp of womanhood, and the slightest upset meant the end of the world for her.

"Can you call Brenda and tell her there's been a change of plans?" he suggested.

Rikki poked her head into his office and blinked at him. "I never thought of that."

"Do it quick, the bus will be here in twenty minutes, and it looks like you haven't done your hair yet."

"Okay, thanks, Dad." She gave him a quick peck on the cheek and scampered off.

Neil slumped in his chair. Another teenage crisis averted.

Rikki made it to the bus stop on time, and Neil settled in to working without interruptions for the morning.

Ten minutes after the bus lumbered by the house, the landline trilled and he cursed as he glanced at the caller ID. It was the owner of the magazine he was currently working for, and they only called unless there was something wrong with his work.

What's next? Kelsey being transferred across the country or Rikki causing problems at school again?

His temper started flaring when the magazine owner gave him her opinion on how he could improve his writing, while he bit back the urge to fly into her about changing her mind on what he should write for them several times within a week of the due dates.

He hung up the phone and was about to start rewriting the last article when he heard retching in the hallway.

"Punky, you goddamn idiot. Thanks for putting the icing on the cake of a rotten morning!" he bellowed and threw a stack of papers across the room to alleviate some of his frustration.

At her workplace, Kelsey's day wasn't going any easier. The number nine pump crashed after a customer messed up their prepaid order, someone found a moldy sandwich in the back of one cooler, and she had gotten more complaints about the price of gas than she could remember, all in the three hours since she'd started her shift.

The day's heavy rain didn't seem to deter anyone from venturing out and filling up their gas tanks or coming in for cigarettes or lottery tickets.

Since she was putting in her tenth shift in two weeks, Kelsey had hoped for a slow day, and her wish wasn't being granted. She was slowly getting irritated from dealing with rude people and the day to day technical difficulties one experienced in the customer service industry.

Hardly seeing Neil wasn't helping her disposition. Between her odd hours and his constant deadlines from the demanding owner of a magazine, they'd had only that stolen hour alone, and she didn't know when they would get another one. If they didn't spend time together with Rikki there too, she wouldn't see him at all most days.

She desperately held on to the image of seeing him on her way home as another busy streak began.

An hour later, Kelsey tried catch her breath. "Is it just me, or did the rain bring out all of the rude and stupid people?" she asked Sharon when things settled down.

"I'm not sure what's going on," her boss admitted, "but this is crazier than a Thursday night before gas is rumored to go up a nickel."

"Or even a cent," Kelsey sighed and rolled her shoulders.

"Go get a coffee and sit down for a few minutes."

"Thanks." She headed for the coffee machine.

"Kelsey, there's been a change of schedule," Sharon said.

"Who's sick this time?" Kelsey grumbled under her breath.

"No one. I gave you a few days off to catch up on some rest."

Kelsey turned to stare at her boss incredulously. "It's my

turn to work nights this weekend."

Sharon shrugged and started filling out an order form. "Not anymore. Kathy is working both nights. You're off from Friday afternoon until Tuesday night."

"It's supposed to be her weekend off," Kelsey muttered and sighed tiredly.

"She asked for more hours. I've been giving so many to you over the last while, it's only fair that you get a break while she gets those hours she asked for. Things have been a little hectic for you lately, and you're not doing things you should be doing."

"I don't have time for a social life with a fourteen-year-old daughter."

Sharon opened a drawer, scanned its contents and made a note before she answered. "You could spend more time with Rikki. A girl her age needs her mother, or a good female role model."

"I miss her on days I don't see her," Kelsey admitted.

"Then there's the case of your boyfriend." Sharon peered at her over her glasses. "How often do you see him?"

Kelsey lowered her gaze, a little embarrassed that her boss remembered an offhand remark she made three weeks ago about seeing someone. "With or without Rikki around?"

"Without."

Kelsey let out a long breath and shrugged.

"Who are you dating?"

"It's Neil."

Her boss' eyebrows rose. "Your daughter's father?"

"He adopted her after he married her adoptive mother," Kelsey mumbled.

Sharon nodded slowly and smiled. "He's a nice man."

She grinned. "Yeah, he is."

"Spend some time with him this weekend, and alone if you can do it."

"I hope to, but I don't think we'll be alone."

"That's a shame. Every couple needs to be alone once in a while," Sharon advised. "Go sit down and call Neil. I'll take care of things while you're talking to him."

"Thanks, Sharon."

"You can thank me by getting some rest."

Kelsey did as her boss ordered and stopped at Neil's house on her way home from work that afternoon. To hell with his upcoming deadline—it was either see him or lose her mind.

Five minutes, that's all I ask. I don't care if we get any alone time or not, I have to see him, today.

Luckily, Neil was on a break when she arrived, and Rikki was nowhere in sight. Although he looked tired and there were worry lines etching his face, his kiss in greeting was warm, and it made Kelsey's insides quiver.

"What happened this time?" she asked as they sat down on the sofa together.

"Remember that article I sent in last week? Apparently, it wasn't the quality the owner expected from me. She insisted I rewrite parts of it."

"She changed things up on you ten times in the last week. What a fucking bitch."

"She knows what I thought of it. I told them if she does it to me again, it'll be the last time I do anything for her."

"Hopefully she got the message this time. How is the new one coming along?" Kelsey asked and rubbed his knee with a hand.

"Faster than I had hoped. I should be able to send off the final copy on Thursday afternoon."

"Is Rikki doing her homework?"

"I think she only had some math to do, and that was done on the bus. She's on the phone with Taffy right now," he replied and leaned forward to kiss her as he slid an arm around her waist. "If we're lucky, she'll be a while."

Good. The longer she's on the phone, the better. Kelsey nuzzled her mouth against his and snuggled deeper into his arms. "I only asked to see you for five minutes, even with Rikki around, so this is a bonus."

His mouth covered hers, hard, and his tongue thrust between her lips. She reached up to tangle her fingers into his hair and lost herself in him.

Footsteps alerted them to Rikki's approach.

"I'd better move before she sees us," Neil whispered.

Kelsey nodded and absently hugged herself. "I wish we could tell her."

"Soon," he replied. "I want to keep this between ourselves for a bit longer." He touched her cheek.

She leaned into the caress. "I understand."

Rikki was filled with her usual gossip and updates on upcoming school events. Her constant stream of chatter lasted a full half hour.

Kelsey silently wondered if her daughter took a breath once in a while.

"Dad, did you sign my permission slip?" Rikki suddenly blurted.

He stared at her blankly. "What permission slip?"

Her eyes rolled. "It's for our class trip to Ste. Anne. I told you about it a month ago."

His brow furrowed. "I don't remember that."

"I thought it was next week," Kelsey said.

Rikki jumped up with a sigh and grabbed a paper off the refrigerator. She slapped it on her father's chest and shook her head. "Nope, and if you would have read this, it says this coming weekend. I have to have the slip in tomorrow if I want to go. We leave Friday morning."

He grabbed the paper before it could flutter to the floor. He quickly scanned it and shrugged. "It's definitely this weekend. Why I don't remember — "

"You had a bunch of deadlines over your head, and you were working round the clock," Kelsey muttered.

He nodded and started reading it more thoroughly.

Rikki tossed a pen at him. "Just sign it, Dad."

He scrawled his name and the date on the correct lines. "Where are you going again?"

Rikki rolled her eyes. "We're going to Ste. Anne and other spots around the Annapolis Valley, like Port Royale and Grande Pre."

"When will you be coming home?" Kelsey asked.

Rikki's answer of *Monday* was a distant whisper as Kelsey stared at Neil across the table.

Although his face was impassive, there was a hint of smoky promise in his eyes. It made her insides tremble.

One corner of her lips rose upward in a silent acknowledgement.

Friday.

Her stomach did a flip flop and ideas started zinging through her mind when she saw his nostrils flare slightly. He marginally winked at her behind their daughter's back.

The volume of Rikki's babbling rose to normal, "Anyway, Tania wants to share a room with me, Taffy and Brenda, but Mrs. Lockhart said that we can't share a room with all of our friends. I guess we're getting the new girl in with us," she grumbled.

"New girl?" Neil asked, confused.

"Yeah, her name is Avery, and she's stuck up." Rikki sighed dramatically.

"You mean Avery Knickle? I met her mother the other day, and she said she can't get why no one will talk to her daughter. Avery is really shy, not stuck up, from what I hear." Kelsey narrowed her gaze at her daughter. "Since when did you start judging people for not talking much in class or sitting by themselves?"

Rikki blushed to the roots of her hair. "I, uh. Um," she stammered.

"Um, what?" Kelsey asked with a raised eyebrow.

Their daughter swallowed hard and her face turned bright pink under her parents' scrutiny.

After a minute, Rikki raised her gaze to the ceiling and flung her arms wide in resignation. "I'll talk to her."

"And no complaints if she winds up sharing the room with the rest of you instead of one of your other pals," Neil instructed. "Compromise."

"Geez." Rikki pouted and folded her arms across her chest.

Neil pushed the paper at her. "Don't forget to put this in your book bag."

Rikki grabbed it and ran down the hall.

The instant she was out of the room, Neil came around the table to whisper in Kelsey's ear, "No kids, no phone, no work."

"Just us," she murmured and kissed him softly.

CHAPTER EIGHT

It was Friday morning, and gas had gone up a few cents overnight, which meant only the ones who hadn't heard the rumors about it were coming in to fill their tanks. It had been a quiet morning so far, and wasn't halfway finished yet.

The clicking of the clock above her echoed loudly in the silence of the store. Kelsey shot it a filthy look when she noted only two minutes had passed since the last time she checked.

The coolers were faced and restocked, the floor had been swept and mopped, and the counters were spotless. The only thing she could do to keep herself occupied was check the washer fluid in the tanks and making sure everything was neat and tidy around the pumps.

You did that first thing, and we've done less than two hundred in gas, so there's no point in making sure everything's fine out there. She gave the checkout counter another swipe with her paper towel and with another glance at the clock, wondered if time was going backwards.

Just over seven hours to go until Kathy came in to relieve her.

Without warning, her stomach clenched in longing as an image of Neil and their upcoming rendezvous rose in her mind.

She pushed it away with a grimace. *Keep busy so you're not daydreaming. Thinking about Neil and how Rikki is gone for the weekend is only going to make the time go slower!*

She jumped as the door opened and Sharon breezed in, her carryall bag over one shoulder and her hands laden with various items.

Kelsey immediately rushed to help, grateful for her boss' distraction.

Sharon handed her half of her burden with a smile and nod. "It's been a slow morning?"

Kelsey nodded as she followed her boss back to the office. "I think everyone filled up last night."

They unloaded Sharon's things into the small compartment and her boss stared at the computer terminal as she removed her coat and hung it on the back of her chair. "I may as well start training you for a few more things."

She motioned for Kelsey to follow her, and they walked out into the main area. Sharon grabbed an order booklet as they passed the back counter and opened it.

"I thought I was done with my training," Kelsey said and followed Sharon onto the floor.

"For a general counterperson, you have, but not for things like cigarette, chip and other order forms. It's time you learned all of that."

"Why? You, Kathy and Marjorie do it."

"Kathy will be retiring in a couple of years. We're going to need someone to replace her when the time comes," Sharon replied and handed the book to Kelsey.

She took it with a raised eyebrow. "I thought Jeremy was next in line for that."

"He's only a kid, and I don't see him working here much longer."

"Why not?" Kelsey couldn't keep the shock out of her voice.

"He didn't do anything wrong, if that's what you mean. He's talking about going back to school or moving out west. I'm expecting him to hand in his resignation any day now."

"What about Enid? She's been here for years."

"She told me a few years ago that if I dared to offer her

Kathy's position, she'd quit."

"Enid said that?"

Sharon nodded and pointed to the large book in Kelsey's hands. "You're bored and hoping the day will pass by quickly so you can start your weekend. Let's get to it."

With a sheepish grin, Kelsey ducked her head and started studying the order form.

Neil dropped Rikki off at school that morning. He didn't want her taking her suitcase on the bus, and he wanted to spend a few extra minutes with her before she left the area for three days.

The bus was scheduled to arrive at the school at nine that morning, and it would be heading toward Annapolis Royal before ten. Their first stop was the historical site of St. Anne. Their itinerary included a visit to Port Royal on Saturday, and a final destination of Grande Pre on Sunday.

Although he and Rita had taken Rikki to all three places in her younger years, they had taken the tour in English. This was the first time Rikki was taking the full tour in French. She chirped in excitement as he unloaded her suitcase from the trunk.

"There's Taffy and Ruby!" she exclaimed and ran to her best friend.

Neil watched the two girls jump up and down with a grin on his face. Two young women, with bright smiles, shining hair, long legs and makeup started bopping their hips together in fun.

His smile faded as a spark of surprise traveled through his stomach. The little girl who used to sit on his shoulders with ice cream dripping into his hair during the Canada Day festivities was gone.

Rikki turned to grin at another girl, and Neil saw a flash of the child she had been.

No, she's not gone.

She had grown up into a beautiful young lady who loved rock music, math class, and science fiction novels.

He leaned back against the side of the car with his arms folded across his chest and waited patiently for Rikki to gather up her things and get checked in with her teacher.

Ruby sauntered over after a minute. "Don't worry, she'll be fine. I'll keep an eye on her," she said.

"Yeah, thanks," he replied with a guilty grin. "This is the farthest she's gone on an overnight trip without me."

"She has to have a little freedom."

"I know, Ruby."

She patted his arm and giggled when Taffy almost tripped over thin air. "They're growing up so fast, aren't they?"

"It's way too fast for my liking. I look at them and feel so damn old sometimes."

"I'm a year older than you are, so what does that make me?" Ruby shot back with a raised eyebrow.

"Ancient."

She swatted his arm and snickered. "Kelsey's off this weekend."

"Oh?"

"She may be a little lonely without Rikki around. Why don't you call her?"

He glanced at her warily. *Are you trying to play matchmaker?* "Why?"

"You two need a break once in a while. Since you're Rikki's parents, now would be a good time to catch up on adult stuff with her."

There was a twinkle in Ruby's blue eyes that confirmed his suspicions.

Embarrassed, he averted his gaze, hoping she wouldn't pick up on his anticipation for the weekend ahead.

He moved his focus to the girls, who were standing in a

large circle and talking with their friends who were going on the trip. "Rikki said she likes to write when she's alone. She's been working a lot lately and hasn't had much time to do it. I doubt she'll welcome anything that takes her away from her stories." He kicked a sneaker on the sidewalk and smiled. "I have another project due in a couple of weeks, and I thought I'd get a jump on it while I'm not tripping over a group of giggling teenagers."

Ruby made a non-committal noise and rolled her eyes.

"I may call her tomorrow, if I need a break," he conceded.

She smiled, and her reply was cut off by the first bell of the day.

Everyone with Rikki and Taffy scattered. Ruby draped her arm around Taffy's shoulders and they started sauntering toward the junior high complex.

Neil grabbed Rikki in a bear hug and held her for an extra moment. "Be good, learn a lot, stick close to Ruby, and don't forget to have fun." He gave her a long kiss on the forehead and hugged her one last time.

She pulled away, quickly gathered her things, and started running so she could catch up with Ruby and Taffy. "Call Kelsey," she yelled over her shoulder.

"I will."

She disappeared into the school.

Neil stared at the doors for a long moment, and a shot of sadness zoomed up his spine.

Let her have fun and get home safely, he prayed silently as he climbed into his car.

Kelsey almost flew home at the end of her shift that afternoon. She could barely keep herself from running to her car or from speeding across town.

Slow down, girl, or you're going to get a speeding ticket. Her foot eased on the gas pedal and she drummed her fingers on the steering wheel anxiously when she was stopped at any red lights. A few curses echoed in the cab when she got behind someone who seemed like they were going slower than a snail in reverse.

"Hurry up," she muttered between clenched teeth and almost rear-ended him when he slammed on the brakes at a green light at the bottom of Victoria Road.

Her fingers clenched the steering wheel and she floored her brake pedal. "Jerk!"

It seemed she always got behind some sluggish idiot when she was in a hurry.

"Murphy's fucking Law, and my own rotten luck," she grumbled as anticipation for the night ahead rose in her gut. She had three more hours to wait, but she had a lot of preparations to do before Neil arrived at her place. She wanted to shower, change her clothing, and change the sheets on her bed, for starters. The opening shift started way early to do much other than get up, get ready, down a cup of coffee and arrive before opening time.

What happened after he arrived at her house wasn't planned yet, but Kelsey had a lot of ideas, ones she hoped Neil would like.

Her legs squeezed together and her nipples hardened as a hard jolt of sexual awareness hit her femininity. She inhaled sharply and let it out slowly to calm her overly eager body and mind. Her legs relaxed and she cracked her neck as she stopped at another red light. The slow-moving driver moved into the left turning lane at LaHave Street, and she settled in for the rest of her short drive homeward.

Just a few more hours. If we don't have sex, I'm going to kill him.

The light turned to green and just as she entered the intersection, someone made a right turn in front of her to head up Aberdeen Road, and slowed to a crawl.

"Fucking asshole!" Kelsey's foot floored the brake pedal,

and her loud curse echoed out of the partially opened windows.

A knock on the door five minutes after six signaled the time had come.

Kelsey wiped her damp palms on her denim clad thighs, took a calming breath and straightened her shoulders before she opened the door.

Punky took off like a rocket toward Rikki's bedroom after Neil undid his leash. He stood up and shut the door behind him.

"Hi," she whispered.

"Hey, Kelsey."

The sound of the lock clicking echoed in the room.

She felt awkward as their gazes met.

What if they weren't compatible in bed, or they broke up after a while? She didn't want to lose Neil after waiting so long to be with him. It was a shock to be faced with the chance something could go wrong between them.

She turned to walk into the kitchen. Maybe talking over a coffee would help her relax a little. Her translucent blouse and tight jeans were probably wasted after Punky's greeting and the uneasiness in the room.

Goes to show I'm better off not expecting much, unless I want to get hurt.

She stopped on a dime when Neil's arms locked around her waist from behind.

She turned her head to stare up at him.

He nipped her earlobe as he ground his loins into her backside.

The feel of his granite-hard erection against her buttocks made her pulse accelerate, her breath grow short, and her desire spike. She reached up and back to tangle her fingers in his hair and nuzzled her face against his.

"I thought we were going to wait until later tonight," she

whispered as delight sped up her spine.

"I can't wait for you any longer, Kelsey. I go crazy each time I see you in one of your see-through shirts."

He touched her chin with his free hand. She tugged his head down to hers and their mouths met in a heated, lustful dance. When his tongue thrust deep between her lips, she wiggled her backside against his swollen manhood through their clothing.

He shuddered violently, his arm tightened around her waist and his free hand moved from her throat to an enlarged breast, its nipple puckered in a need that only he could fulfill.

She whimpered into his mouth.

Her free hand started pulling up her shirt, to give him better access. His breathing turned into pants and his arousal seemed to grow as his fingers touched her bare skin.

Their lips parted.

Her head fell backwards to rest on his shoulder and she moaned.

He flicked the nipple and groaned against her ear, "God, you feel so good." He lazily moved his hand downward, away from her breast.

Her hand covered his and tried to move it back up.

He shook it off and moved it out of her reach as he bent his head and nipped the side of her neck.

"Don't stop," she panted.

His fingers brushed her skin above the waistband of her jeans, and his tongue touched her earlobe. "I can't stop," he ground out.

His fingers unfastened the button on her jeans and one slipped between skin and denim. The zipper went downwards, pushed by his knuckles from inside, lace was pushed forward, and slowly his fingers descended toward her most secret place.

She sucked in a deep breath and her hips arched into his

hand, to help him find what he was seeking.

One finger gently slid between her nether lips and touched the spot that would give her the most pleasure. She cried out as her body tensed up, her head on his shoulder, her back against his front and only a strong arm around her waist holding her upright.

"Now, Neil!"

"Not so fast, sweetheart," he said in her ear and moved his fingers to the hair above the slit. "I don't want you coming yet. Save it for when I'm deep inside of you." He shifted his hand to delve deeper into her jeans and slowly started parting the secret folds. His free hand moved to her breast as he found the opening.

A long finger slid inside of her. She squeezed her eyes shut against the onslaught of bliss surging its way through her body.

"So hot," Neil groaned and leisurely pressed the heel of his hand against the front of her mound. "So tight and wet."

"Neil!" Kelsey cried out around a gasp.

She moved her hand to his thigh and upwards, where her fingers touched the fly of his jeans and cupped him.

He shuddered violently and bit her shoulder.

Her fingers pushed through his fly to touch him. *No underwear, perfect.*

In one smooth motion, she flipped his waistband button open.

His arousal felt like hot iron against her hand, and it twitched in response to a stroke from tip to base.

"Bedroom, now," he panted between clenched teeth, and eased his hand out of her.

It was a little awkward walking with her jeans opened, but a quick upwards pull with her free hand kept them from falling. Neil's fingers gripped hers firmly as he followed her to her bedroom.

Nerves bubbled in Kelsey's chest as they stopped by the

bed and stared at each other. The moment had arrived, and she suddenly felt shy despite all of their playing around.

What if I don't please him?

Or worse, what if he doesn't return my feelings?

Her bashfulness and doubts faded when Neil cupped her face in his hands and brushed a tendril of hair out of her face with his thumb before he kissed her softly. His movements were tender, loving, and made shivers travel up her spine.

She put her hands on his chest, and her fingers fumbled several times as she unfastened his shirt and pushed it over his shoulders. His hands dropped to his sides to allow the material to fall to the floor.

A moment later, rough hands yanked her shirt upwards, and their mouths parted long enough for him to pull it over her head.

Somehow, Kelsey managed to push his jeans downward, and although she almost tripped when he did the same to her. The skin-tight denim and lacy panties were yanked off her legs and tossed aside.

His lips covered hers again in a demand for surrender and domination as his arm clamped around her waist. She opened her mouth, thrusting her tongue into his. She let out a soft whimper of surprise when he put his free hand under her ass and lifted her.

"Birth control," she gasped when she felt the head of his shaft pressing against her slit. A shot of pleasure zoomed between her legs into her stomach.

"In a minute," Neil murmured as they fell onto the bed together. "I have to calm down a little, else I'll come all over you. I don't want that to happen yet."

"It'd be okay if you did, I don't mind—" Whatever else she had to say disappeared in a long gasp when he took a swollen nipple into his mouth and drew a circle around it with his tongue. Her fingers tangled in his hair and her back arched in pleasure as he lavished love on one then the other breast and ground his abs against her throbbing core.

Kelsey's excitement soared into the stratosphere and she bit back a scream.

God, it's so hard not to cum when he does that.

Neil lifted his head after a few minutes. "Condom," he gasped.

She reached to her right, found one with her fingers and ripped open the package for him. "Quickly. I need you inside of me."

He swiftly sheathed himself, locked gazes with her, and with a long groan, pulled on her hips.

Kelsey took the cue and wrapped her legs around his waist just before he entered her in a long, swift stroke that had them gasping for breath and sent pleasure shooting through her pussy.

Delight made her cry out and rake her fingers down his back.

Neil rested his elbows on the bed beside her head and thrust his cock deeper into her.

His movements began to speed up, a lot faster than Kelsey anticipated.

God, he must be really horny.

A strong jolt of bliss tore through her core. She held back a scream.

I can't hold off much longer.

"Fuck me harder, Neil!" she yelled between moans. Her head pressed back into the pillow, her back arched, and her sheath clamped tightly around his cock.

His gritty, loud groans in her ear made her pleasure build.

His movements became more controlled, harder, and rougher. It made her entire nervous system tingle in glee, her soaking sheath squeezing him. She could feel his cock getting larger, indicating he was on the verge of exploding.

His tongue thrust deep into her mouth.

Fuck, he tastes so good.

Neil reached between their joined bodies and pressed his thumb against her aching nub.

Kelsey fell over the edge with a scream.

Neil thrust into her one more time and his low shout of male triumph echoed in her ears when she felt his spasms begin.

"Kelsey, I'm sorry it went that fast."

"It's okay."

He sighed. "Normally I can hold back a lot more, but—Christ." The expletive was punctuated by a crick of his neck.

She couldn't hold back a smug grin. "How long has it been since your last lover?"

"I haven't been with anyone since about six months before we found out you were Rikki's birth mother. It wasn't serious. She didn't want to get married again, and I was lonely after Rita passed away. It was friends with benefits." He kissed her forehead and cuddled her closer to his side. "You?"

Her brow furrowed as she tried to remember when her last relationship ended. "It's been over a year, I think." She tried recalling what her now ex-boyfriend looked like and wasn't surprised when no image came to mind.

"What happened to the girl who could remember almost everything?"

She lightly kicked his shin. "It wasn't that memorable." She snuggled closer to his side and thought about the three months she had been with her last boyfriend. "He wanted something that I couldn't give him, so I walked away."

"What did he want?"

She shrugged. "A wife, a home and kids. I don't have it in me to be a wife, let alone to help keep a good home, or be a decent mom to any kid."

"I wouldn't say that, Kelsey. You're doing a great job with Rikki."

"She was almost grown up when she found me, so there's not as much chance of me messing her up now."

"You're not your mother. You don't drink."

"Yeah, but—"

"Drop it. She needs a positive female influence in her life full time, and whether you believe it or not, you're better at it than you think." His fingers trailed up and down her arm.

Tingles of pleasure prickled her skin wherever he touched her.

"Rikki was depressed after Rita died. Her grades were showing it, as was the time she spent with her friends. Only Taffy could get her out into the real world sometimes, and it was like pulling teeth. When we found her adoption papers and the note from her adoptive father, she started coming back to life a little bit. She was a C student before her adoptive mom died, now she's getting almost straight As. Don't you tell me you're not cut out to be a parent. I think you're doing a great job."

She stared up at him with wide eyes and blinked slowly. "I did all of that for Rikki?"

"Yeah."

She rolled her eyes at him.

He tightened his arm around her. "Do you want me to spend the night?"

I don't want you to leave me, ever. "Only if you want to."

He kissed her. "I want to."

"Clothing is optional." She smiled slyly and trailed a finger down his chest.

His fingers toyed with one of her nipples. "You'd better try to get a little rest."

"Why?" It was hard to think when he was touching her like that.

He smiled arrogantly. "You're going to get one hell of a workout once we're rested."

"That sounds like you're planning on wearing me out."

"If you don't wear me out in the meantime."

She nodded. "I'll rest for a bit, if you stay here."

His mouth covered hers in a soft promise. "I'm not going anywhere," he whispered.

Two hours later, warm water rained on their heads and the scent of soap was heavy in the air.

Kelsey leaned back into Neil's chest as he lightly ran a foamy washcloth along the lines of her body. His capable fingers sent shivers of delight through her with each new discovery they located.

Too bad I don't have a large bathtub. It would have been fun to share it.

Maybe we'll do it at his house sometime.

His fingers tangled in the hair between her legs. She gasped and arched her hips forward.

"Do you feel like getting out and going back to bed?" she asked.

"Why? Are you tired?" One finger slid along her slit.

Stop teasing me, Neil.

"No." She turned in his arms, slid hers around his neck and pulled his head down for a kiss. A shot of power zoomed up her spine when she felt his member start to harden against her abdomen.

She pulled back and locked her gaze with his as she grabbed the soap and started running it along his chest, down his stomach, and stopped at the top of the hair that surrounded his member. Her hand moved upwards, slowly and deliberately, toward his chest again and around to his back.

"Whatever you're planning, be careful. It can come back on you," he warned.

Lazily, she slid the bar up to the hair under his arm and down his side. "The only thing that's on my mind is spending time with my guy, and if it happens to be while we're naked, all the better." Her hand moved to his backside and upwards, and she pressed her stomach against his loins to emphasize her point.

"That sounds good to me." He closed his eyes and relaxed under the warm spray.

Kelsey took her time learning the angles and planes of his body, from his shoulders down to his thighs, his back to his front. When her hand cupped him, she noted his arousal and its demand for relief, and how the pouch under it felt heavy.

She glanced at his face and remembered her promise to relieve him a week ago. She dropped to her knees.

Neil's eyes flew open. "What are you—Jesus!" he yelped and let out a long groan as her mouth closed around the head of his aroused flesh.

She flicked her tongue on its tip and locked gazes with him as she took his length into her mouth. Her lips tightened around him and she wiggled her tongue along his underside. He grew larger and harder, he shuddered violently, and a pulse pounded hotly along its length.

He started panting and shoved his cock deeper into her mouth.

She added suction to the exquisite torture she was lavishing on him, then took his balls in one hand and squeezed the base of his erection with the other to make him soar higher.

His knees shuddered against her breasts. "Kelsey, I'm not going last much longer if you don't stop," he ground out around a few harsh pants.

She let go of him and kissed the head of his shaft with a sly grin.

His eyes opened with an evil glint in them.

Oh shit. He warned me, and I didn't listen. What's he going to do, tie me up and make me crazy?

Her slit immediately started pounding in anticipation.

His hands grabbed her under the arms and she felt herself being carried out of the shower, and into the bedroom.

Within seconds, Kelsey felt her comforter against her back.

Neil's gaze locked on hers. He quickly grabbed a condom and put it on.

She tried to sit up, then was forced back onto the bed when he covered her body with his and buried his hard flesh in her welcoming sheath. His mouth crushed hers as he thrust into her roughly, his movements becoming faster and faster as they reached their pinnacle.

Within two minutes, Kelsey cried out in pleasure when her orgasm tore through her.

Neil yelled his pleasure against her neck as he too, came.

"I haven't gone twice in two hours since I was in my twenties. I'm going to be a walking hard-on or dead, at this rate," he joked when he could talk again.

She giggled and pushed on his shoulders. He took the cue and rolled off of her onto his back to stare up at the ceiling.

She curled her body against his side. His arm slid around her shoulders.

"I thought you may want a little help to get going." She sighed contentedly and wrapped her arm around his waist.

"I was ready before you suggested the shower."

She smiled slyly. "I got what I wanted, didn't I?"

He snickered and kissed her nose. "What in the hell is dripping on me?"

Kelsey's head popped up and her eyes widened as she touched her soaked hair. "I think we forgot to turn off the water and dry off. Oops!" She shot out of Neil's embrace and ran into the bathroom.

"Karma's a bitch, Kelsey," he said.

She quickly turned off the water, and grabbed two towels.

"Dry off, you dingbat!" she hollered as she leapt into the doorway.

Her aim was true—the towel hit him square in the face. *Gotcha!*

Saturday Morning
Kelsey's bedroom

Neil traced a finger along the lines of Kelsey's cheekbone as she slept.

She is so beautiful.

He touched her eyelashes, so soft against his fingertips.

Kelsey sighed in her sleep and rolled onto her back.

One bare breast peeked out of the blankets, the nipple level with the rest of the skin.

Neil's mouth started to water when his taste buds recalled how sweet her skin tasted, and his cock hardened with the memory of her moans as he worshipped first one then the other nipple.

The urge to kiss her awake so he could make love to her again rose in his chest, but he pushed it aside.

There will be plenty of time for that later. We had sex three times last night, and didn't get to sleep until late. Kelsey is probably exhausted.

He propped himself up on an elbow and stared down at her.

Her cheeks were flushed in slumber, her thick lashes creating feathery crescents against her soft skin, and her soft, full lips were parted, showing her slightly longer top front teeth. Kelsey's hair was spread across her pillow, the dark brown strands contrasting sharply with her pale pink skin and the pastel green sheets.

She shifted in her sleep, fully exposing her breast.

His cock went from half-mast to granite hard.

God, she has perfect breasts. I could lick them all day and not get tired of it.

He glanced at her face, saw her eyes were still closed, and wondered if she would get upset if he woke her for a quick round.

No, not a quick one. Our first time was fast. She needs to know what it's like to be cherished.

He lightly tugged on the sheet, pulling it down to her waist to expose her chest.

The demand in his loins strengthened.

He blew air across her nipple.

It instantly hardened to a delectable peak.

His entire body reacted to the sight. His pulse quickened, he started to pant, his cock twitched painfully, and his hands fisted in an effort not to crawl on top of her and fuck her awake.

I have to taste her again.

Now.

Neil dipped his head and lazily drew a circle around her nipple with the tip of his tongue.

Kelsey moaned and he felt her touch his head.

Good, I hope she's getting a nice dream from this, starring me.

He shifted so his penis pressed into her hip, then nuzzled his face into her neck.

She smelled fresh, like the aftermath of a rainstorm, but with an underlying layer of springtime and the promise of sex.

She smells perfect.

He kissed the underside of her chin and flicked his tongue against her jawline.

She tastes like heaven.

"Mm. Neil? What's wrong?" Kelsey's voice was soft and husky. She shifted onto her side, facing him. Her hips moved forward, and she hooked her leg over his hip. He felt her tug him closer with her leg.

Oh, god, that feels fucking amazing.

The friction of the down between her legs against the head of his cock was almost too much for Neil. It was taking a lot of control to keep himself from shifting so he could ride her bareback.

She's on the pill, but she'd probably shoot me if I went without a condom.

"Nothing's wrong, sweetheart," he replied. "I was enjoying watching you sleep." He ran a soft line of kisses down her neck to her collarbone, and lingered.

He felt her lower body grind into his hips. One of her hands slid between them and cupped his balls. "I'd say you want to do more than that, going by the size of your cock," she murmured, and gave him a gentle squeeze.

Pleasure zoomed through his balls, into his cock and beyond. "You know me too well," he panted against her chest. He reached up and cupped her breast.

She moaned. "I was dreaming you were going to wake me up by licking me all over, but this is great, too." Her back arched, pushing her upper body into his hands and face. "What do you want to do this time?"

Neil shoved his cock between her legs, grazing the hair hiding her slit, and ran a thumb around an erect nipple. He shifted so he could stare into her eyes. A sudden urge to worship her in the one way he could without her giving back hit him.

"You know what my cock tastes like, I want to taste you. I have to taste you, Kelsey," he whispered and pulled his cock away from her. He then moved his hand downward to cup her mound. He could feel the moisture of her excitement, which dampened his fingers and her pubic hair. He slid a finger between her lower lips and marveled at how wet she was.

He ran a lazy circle around her clitoris with the tip of his finger.

Her hips reared forward, pushing into his hand.

"Oh god," Kelsey moaned, and her breathing quickened.

Without moving his gaze from hers, he removed his hand from her mound and brought it to his face.

The musky and sweet scent of her arousal penetrated his senses.

It was the most compelling and invigorating scent he had ever encountered.

His entire body twitched at the olfactory stimulation and his balls clenched in pleasure.

Holy fuck. If that's not what Heaven smells like, I don't know what does.

Their gazes locked for several long moments. The only sound in the room was their energized breathing, with an occasional hitch in hers.

Kelsey licked her lips.

Neil couldn't take it anymore. He moved downwards, his mouth and tongue seeking their target.

He felt Kelsey's hands guide his head as her leg hooked over his shoulder.

Soft, wet hair rubbed against his face, and the smell of her eagerness penetrated his entire being.

His tongue thrust between her nether lips and found her clitoris.

Kelsey's loud cry of pleasure echoed in his ears.

If asked, Neil could only use one word to describe how Kelsey's pussy felt and tasted.

Paradise.

She wriggled against him, moaning as he nuzzled his face deeper into her most secret spot.

His cock scraped against the sheet, which sent a shot of delight along its length.

Oh god, this is the most amazing thing I've ever tasted.

He flicked his tongue against her clitoris several times, each one harder than the last.

Kelsey's hips rose off the bed, her cleft squashed against his face.

"Oh fuck! I'm going to—Neil!" she cried and stiffened.

He kept lapping at her lower lips, savoring her taste.

She let out a long, high pitched shriek, bracing her feet on the bed and rearing her hips up high.

Neil pulled back when she started to relax and hid a smug smile against her thigh.

He made a mental note to pleasure her with his mouth a lot in the future.

She wasn't the only one who enjoyed it.

Her heady scent still hung heavy in the air, and her taste lingered on his tongue, making him aware his own arousal was stronger than ever.

He shifted so he was on his knees and stared down at her, unashamed his cock was sticking straight out and heavy with excitement. She lay sprawled on the bed, completely open to him, and a long wave of lust overtook him.

Kelsey licked her lips.

He twitched when he felt something against his balls.

"Come here," Kelsey whispered and tugged on his leg with her hand.

With a lazy grin, Neil did as he was told.

Her dark eyes stared up at him as she kissed the head of his manhood.

Pleasure shot down his length. He let out a long breath and touched her cheek. "What's on your mind, Kelsey?"

There was a smoky promise of something in the look she gave him. "Fuck my mouth, Neil."

Her lips closed around him, so soft, wet, and searing hot.

"Oh, god," he groaned and shoved his entire length into her mouth.

Delight tickled every single nerve ending along his cock.

Her fingers cupped his balls and gently squeezed them.

Neil gasped and thrust his hips forward, which matched Kelsey's action of bobbing her head.

She repeated the action each time he moved, and Neil felt the sexual tension building in the head of his cock.

Her tongue flicked the head several times, and he wondered if she was tasting his precum. He had to be leaking some — he was on the verge of exploding.

Each time she moaned or tugged on his balls sent shocks of delight through him. Combined with his red-alert arousal before she touched him, he knew it wasn't going to last long.

The warning tingle hit him hard, and he could feel the pressure building in his cock.

"Kelsey, gotta cum," he ground out and started fucking her mouth hard.

She moaned in reply, the buzz of her voice vibrating his entire length and into his balls.

It was the last straw. Neil fell over the edge with a long, loud shout of masculine triumph, his cock deep in her mouth as he ejaculated.

This is it. I'm a goner. No one will ever be as good as Kelsey. I will never regret loving her.

CHAPTER NINE

Monday

Rikki chattered for hours after they picked her up from school. She was so absorbed in recalling every single detail about her class trip that she didn't seem to notice her parents staring at each other a lot, or how Kelsey snuggled closer to Neil's side when they were on the couch together as they listened to her ramblings.

Neil finally shooed her off to bed an hour early, after noting she'd yawned six times in less than five minutes. For once she said goodnight and wandered into her bedroom without an argument.

"Do you know if she's going to Taffy's this weekend?" Kelsey asked the instant Rikki was out of earshot.

"Not yet. I think the girls are too tired to think much, let alone make plans."

His mouth brushed hers, and Kelsey's desire started to spike. All it took was one touch, one kiss, or a long, knowing stare to get her wet in a demand to have him naked and thrusting into her. Spending an entire weekend having sex had intensified it.

Her hand touched the fly of his jeans. Another surge of power rose in her chest when she felt him harden in response.

"Don't," he whispered and shoved her hand away.

She smiled smugly. "Sorry, I can't help myself. I've been wet since Friday and can't seem to get rid of it, no matter how many times you take me." She deliberately reached down

103

again, cupped him and ran her thumb along his length.

He shuddered, covered her breast with a hand, and nipped her lower lip. "I know, and no matter how many times we do it, I'm still horny too."

A thump echoed up the hallway into the living room. Kelsey jumped and moved her hands to her lap as Neil straightened.

"We have to get it under control again, especially when she's home," she gasped around a wince. "I thought after this weekend, things would be a little calmer, now that we have the first blast out of our systems."

"I won't get any work done on your days off at this rate."

She grinned evilly and said, "Thursday," with a smoky promise underlying her voice.

"If both of us are child free this weekend, you're spending it here."

The thought of another weekend together had her blood thumping and her pussy throbbing with need again. "I'm on days, so I can sleep here."

"I'll make some room in one of my closets for your stuff. If we're going to be spending weekends together at either place, it wouldn't hurt to have a small stash of extra clothing."

"That's not a bad idea," she added with a grin.

He mirrored the smile. After a moment, his face sobered. "It's going to feel weird waking up in the morning without you beside me."

"Same here. I'm used to it now, and a part of me can't wait to let Rikki know what's going on so we don't have to sneak around," she whispered and touched his lips with her fingertips. "I know it's for her good that we do it, but–"

"It's a pain in the ass. We should start dropping hints we're more than close friends. I don't like keeping stuff from her. My sex life isn't her business, but she knows you and loves you. I'd rather let her know we're together."

"You didn't let her know you were seeing that other lady?"

"No. I don't think she would have understood that even though I missed Rita something fierce, I'd probably start dating again at some point." He shook his head. "You're the only one out of the few women I've seen since Rita died that I want Rikki to know about."

She nodded and the tingle at the back of her mind started nudging her again. She shoved it away and kissed him softly. "Is it because I'm her mother, or is there another reason?"

He kissed her hard. "I'd want her to know even if you weren't her mother, Kelsey. You were always special to me, and it's gotten stronger since you've moved here."

She straightened. "Neil, what are you trying to say?"

He cricked his neck. "I don't know. However, I don't think it's the right time to go down that road." He stared at her tenderly and trailed a finger along the bridge of her nose with a smile. "When I'm ready, I'll tell you."

Kelsey nodded. "How and when do you want to drop hint number one on our daughter's head? We have to make it subtle, but something she'll pick up on."

"You used to do editing for others at the shelter. Why don't you can come over and edit my stuff? You can be at the house after school, and we can slip her that tidbit without getting into trouble."

"Neil, I'm not sure how good my editing is these days. It's been a while. I haven't written anything since I left the province."

He frowned. "You stopped writing? Kelsey, you were great at it."

"I didn't have the time, or the urge," she mumbled, ashamed she'd broken her promise to him not to give it up after she moved away.

"You're going to get back into it. Do I have to duct tape you to a chair with a notebook or computer until you start?"

She gave him a shove. "Do it and you'll be in deep shit, mister."

"If you mean a night or a whole weekend of me submitting to your every whim in the bedroom, I'll gladly do it."

A slow, goofy grin spread across her face. "I like the idea of having you as my sex slave."

"It wouldn't be slavery, because I'd be more than willing to do whatever you want, as long as I can worship you the entire time," he whispered.

Her sheath instantly tightened and dampened. With a firm, mental reminder their child was in the house and could easily overhear their conversation or see them, she lightly elbowed his ribs and hissed, "Control yourself, unless you want our girl getting an early education."

Neil jumped, darted his gaze around the room and nodded with a sheepish grin. "Do I really have to save it for Thursday?"

"Yeah, unfortunately," she muttered and they exchanged a mournful glance.

Wednesday was an opening shift that went into the mid-afternoon. It was a busy day, due to unusually warm temperatures and sunshine for late March. The residents of Lunenburg County were slowly coming out of their winter hibernation.

After her shift ended, she went home to change before she went over to Neil's. She was anxious to see him and their daughter.

When she unlocked the door, Kelsey heard a noise from the hallway.

That didn't sound like one of the cats.

Shit. I hope someone didn't break in. I'll fucking shoot them if they did.

Warily, she grabbed an umbrella and held it like a baseball bat. She crept down the hallway, toward the bathroom.

There was a loud thump from her daughter's bedroom. The door was shut. She couldn't see what or who was in there. She froze, ready to swing, and held her breath as the doorknob turned.

Her daughter jumped and yelped when she saw Kelsey.

"What the fuck?" Kelsey screeched. She slumped against the wall, the umbrella dropped to the floor, and she covered her heart with a hand.

"Kelsey, are you okay?" Rikki asked, her eyes huge.

Kelsey tried to catch her breath. "I thought you were a burglar!" she exclaimed and slid down the wall to land on her rump. "You scared the shit out of me."

Rikki slapped a hand over her mouth. "Sorry!"

"I'm glad it's you." She shook her head rapidly and let out a long breath. "Give me a second to get my bearings, and you can tell me why you came over without calling first."

Rikki nodded sheepishly and helped her mother stand. "I'll make you some coffee while you change."

Kelsey waved her off and went into her bedroom to change out of her work clothing and into her usual home clothing of jeans, a t-shirt and sneakers.

Did something go wrong at school, or did she have a fight with her father?

Hopefully whatever it is, I can help her. If not, we may have to recruit Neil.

Or, if it's really bad, Gina and Ruby too.

Rikki was at the table, mournfully staring into a glass when Kelsey entered the kitchen a few minutes later. She brushed a hand over her daughter's hair and sat down.

"Did you and your dad have a fight?" she prompted.

"No," the girl whispered.

Whew, I hate seeing them argue. "Call him to let him know where you are."

"Can we wait a bit?"

"Call him, or I will."

"You do it. He'll freak out on me for sneaking out of the house." Rikki hung her head.

"I'm willing to let it go, as long as you spill why you did it," Kelsey said. "I'll try to convince your dad to let it pass too, but you'd better get ready to start singing."

"Yes, Ma'am." Rikki got up and went into her room.

Kelsey dialed Neil's number.

"It's me," Kelsey said quietly when he answered. "I'm going to be a bit late."

"What happened, did you get roped in to working a double shift?" Neil sounded a little annoyed.

"No. I'm home." She sighed. "Something came up."

"What?"

Kelsey fell silent as she mulled over how to tell Neil without the expected blow up. *He has a long fuse, but not when it comes to Rikki. It's like touching a lit match to gasoline.*

"Kelsey, what happened? What's wrong?" The amount of concern in his voice made her heart skip a little.

No time for that. Tell him.

"Rikki is here," she blurted.

"No, she's not. She's in her room, listening to music."

Kelsey sighed again. "Go check."

"I'm not going to check."

"Please, go look in her room. You'll see I'm telling the truth."

He let out an irritated noise. "I'll check, but you're going to feel foolish when you hear me talking to her."

Wrong. She could hear the music blaring over the airwaves. *I'm going to really let her have it for making him think she was still home. God.* She picked at a cuticle while she waited.

A moment later, Neil bellowed, "The fuck?"

"She's not there, is she?"

"No. Where is she?"

"She's here. She's reading while I talk to you."

"What is she doing over there without my permission?"

"I'll talk to her, and tell you later."

"That's not good enough. She knows not to do this. I'm going to fucking ground her for a month for this!"

"Neil, take a deep breath. She's fine, and promised not to do it again."

"She knows she's not allowed doing that, Kelsey."

"She looks like she's about to cry and decided to talk to me for a change. Let me find out what's going on before you go berserk on her."

"Jesus Christ. Now I see why so many of her friends' parents are going grey."

Neil's grumble echoed in Kelsey's ear. "For fuck's sake, calm down, or I'll kick you in the ass. I can see why she came to me if you're going to react like this each time she does something stupid."

Silence ricocheted over the line. Finally he let out a long breath and cleared his throat. "Good point."

"I'd rather have her sneak out to see me instead of a boy."

Neil groaned. "You're right. Thanks for calming me down. I'm still fit to ground her, but not until we find out what's going on."

"I'll fill you in after I walk her home. We can decide if she needs to be punished or not."

"As long as she's not pregnant, I may let it slip this time."

It was Kelsey's turn to groan. "Now you have me worried. Gee, thanks."

Kelsey called Rikki into the living room after saying goodbye to Neil.

They curled up on the couch together. The cats gladly hogged their laps, two warm, comforting and purring bodies that seemed to calm Rikki.

Kelsey hugged her daughter and prompted, "What's up?"

Rikki averted her gaze and fingered Casey's fluffy black

tail fur with a shrug.

"You risked your father's wrath by sneaking out to talk to me. Spill it, or I'll ground you."

Rikki's eyes rolled dramatically before her head fell to Kelsey's shoulder. "Some of the kids in school are saying nasty things about me."

Kelsey silently cursed the rumor mill at the school, and the viciousness teenagers had for their peers. "What are they saying?"

"They said I lied about my mother, and she wasn't really my mother after all."

"What do you mean?" Kelsey asked and her gut clenched. *Has the truth about Rikki's past come out, and if so, who spilled it?*

Rikki sniffled. "They know my other mom adopted me, and Dad isn't my real dad."

Uh oh. Kelsey's stomach did a back flip and she sighed. "Who did you talk to about me?"

"Taffy, Leanne, Brenda, Carrie and Tania, and Taffy's moms know."

"Did you talk about it anywhere that someone else may have overheard you?"

"Taffy and I talked about it at her place a few times." Her eyes widened and she stared up at Kelsey. "Tim asked me the other day if you were my real mom, and when I didn't answer him, he laughed in my face."

"He may have overheard you and Taffy talking, or her mothers. Do you know why he'd do something like that?"

"He's a jerk. You know how mean he is to Taffy sometimes. Ooh, I'm going to kick his balls so hard they come out of his nose," Rikki groused.

"Now you sound like your dad." Kelsey made a mental note to remind Neil that saying things like that in front of Rikki probably wasn't a good idea.

"Yeah, Dad. He's going to be really mad when he finds out people know you're my real mom, and he's not really my father."

"It's no one else's business. He loves you and protects you, so it's not like it would be obvious he adopted you."

Rikki absently stroked Sammy's tabby-striped head and nodded. "Someone also said I don't know who my birth father was, because you probably don't know either. That really hurt."

Kelsey sighed. "Rumors are carried by people who would like the world to think they know everything, when in reality, they have no clue about anything."

She stroked Rikki's hair and cuddled her closer to her. "I do know who he was, because he was the only boy I had been with before you came along. We were together for a few years, and we –you don't need to know more than that."

"Was he your first?"

Kelsey blushed and wondered if Neil was going to strangle her for being truthful. "Yes, Joey was my first. I loved him, and he loved me too. We were careful, but the birth control failed."

Rikki absorbed it. "I wasn't planned."

"Far from it. He wasn't happy when I said I couldn't keep you, even though we wanted to."

"Your mom was the shits, and you were scared she was going to hurt me too."

"Yes. She was horrible to me, and god knows what she would have done to you." She hugged Rikki tighter and rocked her back and forth.

"If Joey wanted to keep me, why didn't he take me instead?"

Kelsey let out a long breath. "Sweetheart, your father – Joey – didn't have a good handle on life and was in a lot of trouble before and after I got pregnant with you. He was in with the wrong crowd and had a warrant out for his arrest when I went into labour."

"What was that for?"

Kelsey hesitated and took a deep breath before she answered. "It was possession of a controlled substance, with intent to sell."

"He was a drug dealer?" Rikki exclaimed.

"No, a mule. He knew he was holding stuff for others, but didn't know what it was," Kelsey mumbled.

"How did he get into that?"

"I don't know, other than the crowd he hung out with were into that kind of thing."

"So, is he still in jail?"

Kelsey prayed Rikki wouldn't be upset with the truth. "No, he's not."

"Then where is he, and why didn't he come looking for me?"

Kelsey cleared her throat. "He was in jail while he was awaiting his trial, he didn't have the money for bail because his *friends* deserted him and somehow found the stash of money he made from his *work*."

She absently petted Casey while she scrambled to find the gentlest way to tell her daughter the truth about Joey.

"Kelsey? What happened to him?"

"He was in a fight in there, and someone stabbed him with a shank made from a razor and a toothbrush. He didn't make it to the hospital in time," Kelsey whispered distantly.

"He's dead?"

"Yeah."

"When did this—"

"You were a year old."

Rikki started to cry.

Kelsey hugged her close.

"Did he love me?"

"Oh god, yes, he did. He loved you so much that he tried turning his life around, so he could raise you and be a responsible dad, but his friends wouldn't let him. Each time he tried getting away from them, they would threaten to hurt his family, or me. It was either stay in line with them, or risk losing someone he loved."

"Do you know who killed him?" Rikki asked around gasping sobs.

"There was an investigation, and it was done by someone who had ties to his old gang. They found out he was going to come fully clean and decided to shut him up."

Tears started leaking out of Kelsey's eyes as she recalled Joey's mother's horrible screams over the phone line while his older sister told her about his murder. She'd been overwhelmed with grief. He had been her first true love, and they were hoping to get back together when he was released from prison in a few years. To know it wasn't going to happen had ripped her heart in two.

She was still grieving for her lost love when she'd met the man who was now raising her daughter, just over a year after Joey's murder.

Neil hadn't just helped her overcome her horrific childhood and helped veer her away from a path of self-destruction. He had healed her heart and taught her she could love again.

"I wish I had met him, to show him what I'm like," Rikki sobbed out.

"He knows, sweetheart. He's with you, smiling and he's so proud of you, just like your mom."

"Do you have a picture of him?"

"Later, when you're able to see it without crying," Kelsey whispered and rested her head on Rikki's hair. "What do you want to know about him?"

"Everything."

Kelsey sighed and nodded. "I met him when I was six years old, at school. His family was poor, but they were good people. That didn't stop him from falling in with the wrong bunch when we were thirteen. He wanted to help his family, so he started doing things for people he didn't know well. He suspected it was drugs and other illegal things, but kept his mouth shut and did what he was told. His mom thought he was making a lot of money by working at a local farm. He was working there, but it didn't pay half of what he was making from being a mule. He hated seeing his mom work long hours at the nearby hotel — she was barely keeping their apartment and keeping her kids clothed and fed. I guess his father died when he was a toddler, from an accident at his workplace."

Kelsey hugged Rikki tighter and continued. "You look a lot like Joey's sister, Shawna, except her eyes are blue, like Joey's were."

Rikki sniffled. "Is she still alive?"

Kelsey sighed and thought for a moment. "The last I heard, she was, but she was living in Alberta with her husband and kids. I think she's a grandmother. She was a few years older than Joey."

"What about my grandmother?"

"Joey's mom, your grandmother Nellie, died a few years ago. It was around your third birthday." Kelsey had cried when she heard the news. She had loved Nellie, and the feeling was mutual. Nellie had treated her like a daughter, something her own mother, Muriel, never did.

"Did she want you to keep me?"

Kelsey wiped a tear off her cheek. "Yes, and she wanted me to go after you when Joey died. She wanted that part of him back in her life. I was still living with my mother at the time, so I said no. Even if I had gone after you, the courts would have ruled in favour of your adoptive parents. I gave up all rights to you when you were three days old, and it was going to stay like that whether I liked it or not. Although your grandmother didn't like it, she understood it, thanks to

Shawna reminding her about the legalities."

"What does Shawna do?"

"She's a lawyer." Kelsey chuckled. Nellie had been so proud to see her surviving child beat the odds and go to university.

"I want to find her sometime."

"I think her aunt still lives in Shelburne. We can call her and ask her if she has Shawna's number."

"That sounds great. I want to know both sides of my birth family." Rikki snuggled closer to Kelsey and yawned.

Kelsey kissed the top of her daughter's head. "We should go see your dad soon. He's probably wearing a rut into the kitchen floor from pacing with worry."

Rikki immediately flew into her dad's arms and started to cry when they arrived at Neil's house. He hugged her and let her cling to him as his gaze met Kelsey's over the top of their daughter's head.

"She's not pregnant, something came up at school that she needed to ask me about," Kelsey explained.

"What was it?"

"Her birth father," Kelsey mouthed.

He cringed and motioned for her to come closer. When she put an arm around their daughter, he slid one arm around Kelsey's waist and pulled her against his side, forming a comforting circle for their girl.

When Rikki was calm enough to speak, they moved to sit on the couch, with Rikki between them. Kelsey met Neil's gaze over the top of Rikki's head.

He reached behind Rikki and touched her cheek. Kelsey leaned her head into the soothing caress and closed her eyes as her fingers covered his to silently say she was managing.

"What happened?" Neil finally asked.

Haltingly, Rikki told him everything with Kelsey's help.

When they were finished, he let out a long sigh. "I want you to remember there is no shame in being adopted, by me or your mother. Adopted kids wind up with people who want them, instead of having parents who don't care and treat them like your grandmother treated Kelsey."

Rikki nodded. "Yeah."

"I think you wound up in the right place," Kelsey said. "From what your dad tells me, your mom adored you, and I don't think you could have a better dad." Her gaze met Neil's.

Our situation also brought us together.

He gave her one the smiles that made her knees weak and her heart trip over itself.

"Now that you know the truth, you and your friends can start letting people know that you do know who fathered you, if you want," he suggested.

"Tell Taffy first, and I'll give you a picture of him so you can show her."

"Thanks, Kelsey." Rikki averted her gaze and sighed. "Am I in trouble?"

"I'm not overly happy about you sneaking out on me," Neil stated.

"Yes, sir," the girl mumbled. "What am I getting this time?"

Neil and Kelsey exchanged a glance and she replied, "Nothing."

Rikki's gaze darted between them warily. "I'm not in trouble?"

"Not this time, but if it happens again, you're grounded for a month," he scolded. "From now on, you let me know if you're going to Kelsey's house for any reason at all, and the same goes if you're at her house and you're coming over to see me."

"Deal?" Kelsey asked.

"Deal!" Rikki blurted. "Can I call Taffy now? I promised her I would."

"Is your homework finished?" Kelsey eyed her suspiciously.

"No, I had to see you before I did it," Rikki mumbled. "I'll go finish it now."

The instant she was out of the room, Neil leaned over and whispered in Kelsey's ear, "I think she needs both of us right now."

"Agreed. I'll go home, pack enough clothes for a few days and round up the cats. They won't like it, but I'd rather have them pissed off at me instead of not being here in case she needs me too." She glanced at him. "I should bunk with her."

"Fuck."

"We agreed it's in her best interest."

"Yeah," he grumbled.

"We may get a little private time after she's asleep. It's not like we're the first set of parents to have sex with a child in the house."

"Where are we going to do it? In the backyard for the neighbors to see? She'll know if you're in my room, Kelsey."

"We'll figure it out. Try to think of a good spot where we won't get caught and she won't hear us if she happens to wake up."

"Great, we'll be doing it on Punky's sofa downstairs."

"You mean the filthy one he loves to lay on after a mud bath?"

"You got it."

Kelsey gagged. "Yuck. I was thinking about your car. It's in the garage, right?"

He raised an eyebrow. "I haven't had sex in the backseat of a car in years."

"Neither have I, but you have to take what you can get sometimes."

"Since you're spending the night here, we'll do the first round of editing tomorrow."

She raised an eyebrow at him. "Is that your way of saying we'll be spending the day in bed?"

His goofy grin was her answer. "By the way, when you're packing for tonight, don't forget to bring extra clothes for the weekend so Rikki doesn't see it. She'll be at Taffy's house for two nights, and I plan making the most of it. Not that you'll need a lot of clothes." He bit her earlobe.

Suddenly shivering with desire, she met his gaze. "Understood, and ready when you are."

Chapter Ten

Neil and Kelsey tucked Rikki into bed that night, something Kelsey had never seen him do. Although Rikki was fourteen and independent, Kelsey knew they both understood that once in a while, she still needed her parents' reassurance they were there.

Kelsey had also picked up on Neil's need to have the reminder that although Rikki was on the cusp of womanhood, she still needed his love, protection and guidance. She wasn't surprised to see him hover over their daughter for a few minutes after the girl climbed into bed and he gently folded the blankets around her.

"We'll be up for a while, so don't worry about waking either of us if you have a dream or anything." Neil stroked Rikki's hair reassuringly.

"Yeah, your dad wants me to do a double check on his last article for him, to be sure he didn't miss anything," Kelsey added softly and rubbed her daughter's arm. "I'll try to be quiet when I come to bed."

Having her mother sleeping in the same room that night seemed to help Rikki calm down. "Thanks, Kelsey," she whispered, then sighed as she snuggled deeper into her blankets.

They kissed their daughter goodnight and let her settle into slumber.

In the hallway, they stared at each other awkwardly. For several minutes, Neil heard only silence from Rikki's room.

"What are we going to do while we wait for her to fall asleep?" Kelsey asked in a whisper. "She may need us, and—"

"We'll pass the time doing exactly what I told her. I'll run off a copy of the last article, and you can read it while I make the necessary changes on the computer."

"Neil, I'm not sure my editing skills are up to par—" she softly protested as he led her into his workspace.

"Then you can practice on something else, like your writing, before you help me," he replied firmly. "You brought your notebook, didn't you?"

"Yes, but—"

"Get it. I left your bag by the front door so you wouldn't have to disturb our girl if you wanted to work before you went to bed." He sat down at his desk and opened the necessary programs.

"Go," he ordered when she didn't budge.

With a roll of her eyes, Kelsey did as he commanded.

Neil grinned evilly behind her retreating back and jumped when a fluffy, black and white ball of fur landed on the computer desk. His gaze met Casey's deep green eyes and with a sigh, he reached out to give the feline a scratch on the chin. Casey leaned into his hand and purred.

"I can put him out if you want. He may lie on the keyboard and be in your way," Kelsey suggested as she walked back into the room with her notebook and a pen in hand.

"He's fine," Neil reassured her, "It's nice having a cat in here again, and I missed it."

She snickered and leaned forward to see what was on the screen. "Is this the one you're about to send in?" She started skimming it, then pointed to the first line. "You spelled *start* perfectly. Don't you mean *star*?"

He glanced at it, made the necessary corrections, and raised an eyebrow at her. "Who says your editing skills are not great?"

"That was only one line, Neil. I may miss a lot more along the way. Scroll down please."

He hit the print command instead, and the printer whirred through its sequence. When it was finished, he stood up and collected the papers.

He turned back and saw her gaze was on his ass.

He waved the papers in her face. "Get your mind out of the gutter, Kelsey. We have another hour to wait, and this shouldn't take more than that."

"Jerk," she muttered and took the stack from him to survey.

Kelsey was having a hard time focusing on the work with him so close. Each time their arms brushed or they glanced at each other, it became tougher for her to focus on the task at hand. The smell of Neil's aftershave was a siren's call, and the sound of his voice made goosebumps rise on her arms.

She was addicted to this man, and everything about him.

Clearly, Neil couldn't keep his eyes away from the dip at the front of her low-cut t-shirt. When she caught him staring at it, her nipples tightened despite the heat in the room, and her sheath started to moisten.

Kelsey grinned and flicked her gaze down to the crotch of his jeans, which showed the tell-tale bulge of his desire for her. A long rush of desire ricocheted through her, and her body's pleas for release started overriding her common sense. She was almost drowning in her need to surrender to him and dominate him at the same time.

It took a lot of effort to turn her gaze back to the stack of papers on her lap.

Neil cleared his throat and said, "Page two, paragraph five."

Kelsey flipped back to it and put the tip of her pencil on the area in question. "What about it?" she asked without looking at him.

His voice was softly hoarse as he answered. "The third line. Does it sound right to you?"

She read it out loud and frowned. "Maybe it is a little wordy. Let's try it another way and see how it works." She made a few suggestions, and it took a minute for them to find the right way to condense the material into a much shorter sentence.

While Neil was staring at the screen and typing up the edited version of the paragraph, her gaze followed the lines of his jaw, the shadows on his face, the curve of his eyebrow and the flow of his neck to the planes of his chest.

She looked up to meet his gaze, and a trickle of awe went up her spine. When he smiled at her, she realized she was still amazed that he had chosen her to be his lover after so many years of pining over him. She leaned her arm into his and her eyes closed as he kissed her.

Without thinking, she automatically put her hand on the inside of his thigh and trailed it upwards.

He froze and held his breath as her hand stopped short of touching the taunt denim of his fly.

Kelsey pulled back and moved her hand to her lap. "Too much?" she asked sheepishly.

He glared at her and let out his air slowly. "It could be classed as not enough, if we were downstairs," he muttered.

"We agreed on an hour," she murmured and pointedly shifted her focus to the monitor.

Casey flipped his tail across the screen and she reached up to move it out of their way. As she did so, her breast pressed against his arm.

He stood up, grabbed her by the arm, and dragged her to her feet.

Kelsey barely had enough time to suck in a breath before his hands clamped on her hips, and the thread holding her desire and need snapped as his mouth forcefully covered hers.

Her hands slid under his shirt and her nails raked down his bare back. He shuddered and pulled her tight against the rigid length of his cock in reply.

"Basement?" she panted when he moved his lips from hers to nip at her throat.

"Basement," he confirmed. "Check on Rikki, and I'll get some protection."

Kelsey almost ran to her daughter's room; the fear of waking Rikki kept her movements silent and stealthy. She opened the door a crack, peered in, noted a short shadow twitching on the bed, and relaxed when she heard Punky's loud snore.

She quietly pulled the door shut and cringed as the click echoed in her ears.

An arm clamping around her waist from behind made her feet lift from the floor and a scream freeze in her throat.

The arm disappeared and Neil whispered, "Sorry," breathlessly in her ear.

She tried to catch her breath and leaned backwards into his strength and support. "You could have made a little noise to warn me."

"She's a light sleeper when she has something on her mind."

"Perfect," she muttered through clenched teeth. "Hopefully I didn't wake her when I landed."

"We'll give it a minute or two, and if we hear her moving or talking, we'll go back to editing."

"Yeah." She rested her temple against his jaw and they fell silent as they listened for any signs of life from Rikki's bedroom.

Two minutes later, it seemed safe for them to take a few minutes for themselves. Kelsey took Neil's offered hand and eagerly followed him downstairs to the basement.

"What are we going to do if she wakes up and comes down?" she asked as it hit her.

Neil's grip around her fingers slackened. "Uh, I didn't think about that."

"You've been thinking with the wrong head again, obviously."

He shot her a filthy look and glanced around. "There's a bathroom over on the left wall," he murmured, and tugged on her hand. "If she comes down, you'll hide in there and I'll pretend I forgot something in the car."

"And what's she going to think if she sees you're not wearing a stitch of clothing?" she asked as Neil pushed her backwards against the passenger door of his car.

"Who says she'll see anything?" He grabbed her wrists, lifted her arms and held them steady on either side of her head. His hips ground against hers. "I'm too damn horny to get naked."

Kelsey used the car behind her to brace her body as her feet left the floor so she could wrap her legs around his waist. She pulled him closer with her legs and pushed her throbbing pussy into his granite hard cock through layers of cotton as her gaze locked with his. "Kiss me," she ordered in a pant.

His teeth lightly clamped around her lower lip. As the mixed sensations of pain and pleasure traveled down to her breasts and beyond, she squeezed her legs around his hips, which put pressure on their loins. She stiffened as her climax started to build, then felt him tremble.

He lifted his head. "Put your legs down," he ground out between gasps for air.

Kelsey opened her eyes, and her feet hit the floor with a loud slap when she did as he commanded.

He moved half a step backwards, putting a little distance between them.

She flipped open the button on her jeans and pushed the zipper down. "Back seat or front seat?"

"The back," he answered, opening the door.

She crawled inside and flipped onto her back so he could pull her jeans and panties to her ankles as she shoved her t-shirt to her neck, revealing her breasts. The cool air of the basement penetrated the car's open door, and the draft combined with the heat in Neil's gaze as he stared at her made her nipples harden.

He kept his gaze locked on hers as he quickly unfastened his jeans, shoved them down to his hips and fumbled to don the protection.

He pushed her into a sitting position against the opposite door as he got into the car with her. His elbows resting on her jeans, he reached between her legs, spread her slit open with two fingers, and flicked his tongue along her clitoris.

She stiffened as he lavished love upon her, faster and faster, and when she climaxed, she tasted blood as her teeth bit into the inside of her lower lip to hold back her cries.

He repeated the action a few more times, harder and faster.

Kelsey tried to wiggle away from him as bliss rebounded through her again. Her fingers dug into the back of the front seat. When she tried to push him away with her legs, he elbowed one into the back of the seat and held onto the other with his hand.

She was building toward a third plateau when he pulled back and kissed the inside of her thigh. She sucked in air, closed her eyes, and started to go languid in the aftermath.

He grinned evilly and lazily ran a finger along the line of her cleft. Her hips lifted marginally and her hands pushed on his head. "Are you done yet?" she gasped.

"Nope," he murmured and deftly slid a finger inside of her

as he lowered his head and pressed his tongue against her inner folds.

Her head flew backwards to crack against the window and her entire body went rigid as her muffled scream echoed in the car.

He rose to his knees, yanked on her hips and plunged his member into her still vibrating sheath, the head of his cock pressed against the inside spot that would drive her insane.

The onslaught of pleasure made Kelsey's body tense up. Her sheath clenched around him, and she writhed under him as he did it again. She fisted her hands around the front of his shirt to pull him down to her for a kiss, and her teeth ground together.

She ignored the slap of sweat-dampened skin against skin and the harsh sounds of their combined pants and the reverberations of the car's coil springs squeaking as their mouths crushed together and their mutual bliss rose.

A long moan escaped Kelsey's lips when she reached her pinnacle, and when Neil thrust deeply into her one last time and came with a harsh groan, she fell over the edge again.

Their bodies started to relax and the only sound in the large room was their harsh breathing.

Kelsey pressed her face against his neck and her fingers tangled in his hair. Contentment and satisfaction made her drowsy, and the smell of his body in the aftermath made her feel safe and secure.

Neil kissed her head and tightened an arm around her waist. "Are you okay?" he whispered.

"I feel like I've been hit by a truck." She brushed her lips against his neck, tasted the saltiness of the drying sweat on his skin and sighed. "I thought you were too anxious to wait, so how in the hell did you manage to hang on and drive me up a wall without coming?"

"It wasn't easy, but I wanted to slow things down on my

end, so it seemed like a good idea at the time," he admitted as he shifted to a sitting position and pulled her with him.

She automatically laid her head on his shoulder and put her hand on his chest to feel his heartbeat. "If that was your idea of worship, I approve."

He snickered. "You haven't seen anything yet."

"Mm, wait until it's my turn to give it back to you, because you're not going to be able to walk when I'm through with you." Her eyes opened to meet his gaze and she smiled at him.

"I can't wait for it," Neil whispered in reply and hugged her tightly.

The alarm shrieked, and Kelsey's eyes flew open.

Is it six a.m. already? She hadn't slept much between staying down in the basement with Neil until the wee hours of the morning so they could go another round and tossing and turning because it felt odd sleeping in his house, but not his bed.

She buried her face into her pillow and tried to stretch her legs. Something heavy held them down, and a soft grunt reached her ears.

"Morning, Punky," she murmured and reached out with a hand.

Punky whined softly and slurped her fingers.

"Why don't you go wake up Rikki?"

"I'm awake, Mom," came a voice behind her.

Kelsey yelped in surprise. "What the hell?"

Rikki's head almost cracked the bottom of the top bunk as she flew into a sitting position. "Sorry?" she said sheepishly.

"One of these days, you're going to give me a heart attack. When I came to bed, you were in the top bunk."

"I woke up about an hour ago and couldn't get back to sleep."

Kelsey flipped over on her other side. "You had a nightmare, didn't you?"

Rikki nodded morosely and cuddled up to her mother. "Yeah."

Kelsey understood her child's need to be comforted by a parent after something like that. Since her mother was in the same room with her, she must have decided that although the bunks were small, could easily squeeze in and get the security she needed. "I'm glad I was here when you needed me," she replied softly, and hugged Rikki closer to her.

Her daughter sighed and nodded.

A tap on the door preceded Neil's voice coming through it. "Rikki, are you awake yet?"

"We're up," Kelsey replied, "and we'll be out in a few minutes."

"What time did you come to bed last night, Mom?"

"I think it was around two or so. Your dad and I had a lot to do to get his article up to spec."

"I woke up around midnight and wondered, because you weren't here."

Kelsey's cheeks heated up a little. She'd been downstairs with Neil at that time, in the middle of another round of pleasuring each other. "Sometimes it takes a while to see all of the problems in something like an article or story," she mumbled, "and we're not done yet. Your dad wants me to help him with the new one today while you're in school."

Rikki grinned. "Will you be here when I get home?"

"Probably. I'll probably be here on and off on my days off, editing for your dad."

Hint number one dropped, and before Rikki was out of bed. Not bad.

"All right!" Rikki exclaimed and shot out of bed to get ready for her day.

CHAPTER ELEVEN

Three Weeks Later
Kelsey's House

Barely a knock preceded the door flying open and Rikki flying into Kelsey's bedroom with Punky and Sammy on her heels. "Hi, Kelsey."

"Yikes!" Kelsey jumped a foot out of her chair with a yelp.

Casey, who had been napping on top of her monitor, leapt down with a puffed-up tail, let out a startled meow, and zoomed out of the room.

Rikki jumped backwards a step. "Sorry."

"What the hell are you doing here? Never mind, the time got away from me." Kelsey sighed as she glanced at the clock. It was four-thirty, more than an hour after the school bus had gone by and Neil's workday came to an end. She had forgotten how easy it was to get absorbed in a story, and how quickly the day flew by when she was writing.

"Does your dad know you're here?" Kelsey asked when her breath returned to normal.

"He said to tell you he'll be ready for the editing whip tomorrow," Rikki replied with a grin.

Kelsey mirrored it with an evil glint. "I'm off tomorrow, so that works perfectly."

"You'll be at our house when I get home from school?"

"Probably, and don't be surprised if I spend the night again." They had gotten into the habit of her staying in Rikki's bedroom overnight on the days and evenings that she was supposedly helping Neil with his work, although they were not always at the computer. They would work until they knew their daughter was asleep, then sneak downstairs for a little private time. Later they'd come back upstairs and go to bed. The instant Rikki was on the bus in the morning, they'd head for his bedroom until an hour or so before her afternoon bus arrived.

It was the only way they could spend the night in the same house without arousing their daughter's suspicions of their true relationship.

"I like it when you're there. It's kind of like a sleepover, but with my mom instead." Rikki flopped down on the bed and grinned.

"That it is," Kelsey replied absently as she quickly scanned the last few paragraphs on her word processor. The last sentence didn't sound right.

"What are you doing?" Rikki asked as she too, peered at the screen.

Kelsey tried minimizing the window before her daughter could read more of it. "Um, nothing."

"Nothing, my foot. That looked like a story."

Kelsey's gaze met her daughter's, and her stomach twitched nervously. Her grin was nauseated as she replied, "Maybe."

Rikki's brown eyes widened. "Really? That is so cool. Does Dad know yet?"

Kelsey shook her head. "No."

"Why not?"

"It's just scribbling. I'm not sure if it's going to turn into anything, and I don't want to disappoint him."

"What I saw looked really good, and I want to read the rest of it." Rikki gave her mother's wheeled chair a neat shove and she wiggled her way between her mother and the desk.

Kelsey sighed again and tried to turn off the monitor.

"Rikki, it's far from done and not very good, so —"

Her daughter wedged herself in front of the computer and slapped her hand away. "Tough. Dad said you love to write, and you were good."

Rikki would believe her father if he told her the sun revolved around the earth. "He's saying that to be nice." She narrowed her eyes at Rikki. "How do you know he's upset about that?"

"I overheard him bawling you out for not sending one of your old stories to a publisher," the girl replied smugly and continued reading.

Kelsey remembered the scolding Neil had given her the other day and cringed. "I hoped you wouldn't hear that."

"It's kind of hard not to — he's pretty loud when he's giving it to someone. Wow, keep this," she said and pointed to a paragraph, "it makes me want to know what happens next."

Kelsey saw the excitement on Rikki's face. "Do you like it?"

"I love it."

"I'll have to finish it, even if you're the only one who reads it," Kelsey grumbled jokingly.

"Dad has to read it, too. And Taffy, and her moms," Rikki exclaimed. "This is too good not to share with everyone."

Kelsey resigned herself to having her work critiqued by the entire neighborhood. "Rikki, I swear, if you're only saying that because I'm your mother —"

"I know what I like, and this is awesome."

Kelsey let out a long breath. "You can tell your dad, and Taffy, on the condition you don't get mad at me if I don't get it published."

"Aw, Kelsey."

She held up a hand. "I haven't written in a long time, and this may not be great when it's finished. It's in rough draft."

Rikki scoffed. "It's better than some of the published stuff I've read through the school. Don't lie to me." She primly turned back to the monitor and her grin widened.

"No dreams about me hitting the best seller list."

Rikki shushed her with a wave of her hand.

Kelsey glared in reply.

Her secret was out, and although she knew Neil was going to be pleased, it still sent a surge of anxiety through her.

What if I don't have what it takes to make it as a writer?

"Neil, that last article was almost perfect," the owner of the magazine said the following morning. "Other than adding a couple of commas and shortening a sentence or two, we didn't have to do much to it to make it ready for publication. Fantastic job."

"Uh, thanks," he mumbled and shifted the phone higher on his shoulder, a little thrown off by the praise. Rhonda Johnson was tough to please, and only his need to pay the bills and keep a good home for his daughter had kept him from telling her off on several occasions.

"It's the best work I've seen from you, and you're one of the top freelancers out there. Did you have help with it?"

He leaned back in his chair and grinned. Neil couldn't wait to tell Kelsey that her revisions were almost exactly what Rhonda wanted. "My girlfriend does all of my editing."

"Oh?" Rhonda's voice rose, an indication her curiosity was peaked. "Is she another freelancer like you are, or a professional editor? She's good."

"No, she's not."

"What does she do?"

"She works at a gas station, as a cashier, but she writes in her off time."

"I see. What does she write?"

"I think she's trying to write a short story."

"What genre is it?"

Neil wondered why Rhonda was interested in Kelsey's

work. She wasn't one to be interested in anything other than her staff, temporary or not, and giving long, overblown critiques. "I haven't read it yet, but my daughter has seen parts of it."

"It might be young adult, if she's letting your daughter read it," Rhonda murmured. He heard her shuffling papers over the airways. "Do you think she would allow me to review it?"

His eyes widened. "I'm not sure if she'd let you see it. She's pretty shy about showing her writing to anyone outside of Rikki and me. Why?"

"We're going to start a new column this winter. It's going to feature stories written by unpublished authors, and I want the first story to be in the young adult genre, to get teens buying the magazine."

"It's not finished yet, and she's only writing it because she loves —"

"Sometimes the best writers are the ones who don't want to be published, yet still have the passion for it, like your girlfriend," Rhonda interrupted. "Can you talk her into sending me part of it for review? It's okay if it's in rough draft. The deadline for the first author isn't until September."

"Rhonda, I don't think I can do that. Kelsey is pretty damn closed mouthed about —"

"Oh, posh. If she says no, you can just send me a copy on the sly, right? What's her last name?"

"Wagner," Neil mumbled and wondered if Rhonda had painted him into a corner. "She'd kill me if I did that."

"She'll get over it. Get a copy of her work, and send it to my email when you get a chance. After you do that, I'll be glad to send you another assignment, with a big bonus for helping us. If you don't, well, we may not be interested in working with you any more. I know you don't have any other magazines sending you offers, and work has been slack for some of you lately."

The threat of losing contracts with her magazine set Neil's teeth on edge. She was right—outside of doing a number of articles for her, there hadn't been much in the way of freelancing contracts available in his field of expertise the last few months. If Rhonda hadn't offered to take him on for a temporary position, he would have been struggling to keep the house and feed his daughter.

He cringed at the thought of Kelsey losing her temper at him for going behind her back once she found out he had given this bitch a copy of her writing, even after he explained what happened.

"I'll send you some of her work. Give me a day or two," he muttered between clenched teeth.

"Have it in my inbox by Monday at the latest. If it's not there, I'll assume you found work elsewhere," Rhonda replied briskly and hung up.

Neil's body deflated, and he wondered how long he was going to live after Kelsey found out.

As long as I don't lose her. I'd rather die at her hands than let her go this time.

Sunday morning, Kelsey woke up to soft kisses along her cheekbone. She snuggled closer to Neil, smiled and sighed happily as his arms tightened around her.

Paradise.

Reality struck when she opened her eyes to smile up at him and saw the sun peeking through the curtains. She grimaced, squeezed her eyes shut and pressed her face against his neck. "Is it morning already?"

"It is." There was a little disappointment in his voice.

"Time goes by too fast when you stay over. How late is it?"

"It's just after nine. I can stay a little longer if you want."

Kelsey lazily ran her fingers up and down his side. "I'd

love it, but don't you have to beat Rikki home?"

"I probably won't see her for a few more hours," he said and kissed her.

She nuzzled her face against his and reached down to stroke him. She heard him groan a second before his mouth covered hers, hard, and he thrust his hips forward and his hand covered one breast.

Between heated kisses, she murmured, "One for the road?"

"Or two, if we're quick," he replied against her lips.

A soft bark from another part of the house halted their movements.

"What did he get into now?" Kelsey whispered irritably.

She listened carefully and when the noise wasn't repeated, Kelsey relaxed.

"He's probably trying to play with the cats, or one of them got in his way," Neil murmured.

"Probably." She tangled her fingers in his hair and tugged his face down to hers as her back arched in silent invitation.

She felt him move. One arm left her side and a blast of cooler air brushed her nipple. She could hear the rustle of plastic in her ear when his hand brushed her face.

He must be anxious if he has a condom already.

She wriggled her hips upward and moaned against his ear.

He rolled on top of her. His erect cock brushed the hair on her mound, sending tingles of delight into her core.

"Hurry, Neil," she whispered and deliberately ground her pussy against him.

His chuckle reverberated against her chest and he kissed her. "You are an anxious little thing in the mornings, aren't you?" There was a teasing note in his voice.

"Only because you know how to make me cum, and fast." She reached down and grabbed his ass cheeks, one in each hand, massaging them.

His pleased growl made a surge of power rise in her chest. *He's putty in my hands. I love it.*

Punky barked again, this time more excitedly, followed by steps coming down the hallway.

"Kelsey? Are you awake?"

Kelsey froze and stared at Neil in shock as Rikki's voice echoed through the door.

Neil's jaw clicked nervously.

No. She's not here.

"Kelsey?"

Oh fuck, she IS here.

The sound of footsteps coming closer sank into Kelsey's brain and freed her surprise. She slapped a hand over Neil's mouth and hissed, "I'd better say something before she walks in."

He nodded. His eyes were huge.

Kelsey felt his penis go flaccid against her slit. *Yeah, my urge to have sex kind of disappeared too, Neil. Talk about a great way to ruin the party. Thank heavens we shut the door last night, or we'd be up the creek right now.*

"Rikki? Is that you?" Kelsey called out softly.

The footsteps stopped just outside of her bedroom and the couple tensed as they prayed their daughter wouldn't walk in without permission.

"Yeah, it's me," Rikki grumbled through the door.

"What are you doing here so early? I thought you were at Taffy's."

Neil shifted off of her and she covered his head with the duvet.

She prayed her daughter wouldn't hear it, or if she did, assume she was getting out of bed.

The girl let out a long, disgusted sigh. "Taffy's brother fell off his bike and they took him to the emergency room. His arm looks funny, and he screams every time anyone touches it."

So that explained why her daughter had left her best friend's house so early.

"Ouch," Kelsey absently replied and scooted away from Neil. "Let me get dressed, and you can tell me about the sleepover. There's some juice and water in the fridge if you're thirsty."

Rikki was quiet for a moment, and Kelsey prayed her daughter would take the prompt. "I'll be in the kitchen." Her footsteps faded as she scampered off.

Neil groaned in his spot under the covers. "That was close," he murmured.

Kelsey grabbed her robe off the back of the chair and stood up to slide it on. "We're not out of the woods until she's out of here, so stay put and keep your yap shut," she hissed softly as she tied the belt. "I'll try to think of a way to get her out of the house without seeing you, so be ready to go at any time." She leaned down and gave him a quick kiss. "I'll be fast, I promise."

Kelsey cracked the door, checked the hallway and relaxed when she saw Rikki wasn't within eyeshot. She crept through the door and shut it firmly behind her before she walked out to the kitchen.

Rikki was pouring a fresh glass of fruit punch when her mother entered. She gave Kelsey a sheepish grin and mumbled, "Sorry I woke you."

Kelsey kissed her cheek in greeting. "I've been awake for a while, thinking about the next twist in the story. I was going to get up and start writing when you arrived. Don't apologize."

The girl beamed at her and carried her glass of juice to the table to flop down on a chair.

Kelsey started to make coffee. She needed one shot of caffeine to help her wake up and think of ways to get her daughter out of the house quickly. "Did you have fun last night?"

Rikki nodded excitedly. "Yeah, it was great until Tim

decided to be stupid."

"What did he do this time?" She set the coffeemaker running.

"He was trying to hop his bike on Ruby's car and fell off."

"Yikes. That's the third time he's hurt himself this year?"

"Fifth." Rikki rested her chin on a hand with a disgusted noise.

Kelsey let out a long sigh and shook her head. "That boy has no fear, I swear." A soft thump from the bedroom area alerted her that Neil was getting dressed and must have tripped over something in his haste.

Maybe making some noise won't hurt. "Do you want me to do your laundry? I was going to toss a load in."

Rikki nodded. "Thanks. I'll get my bag." She hopped up and ran to the entryway.

Kelsey hoped the washer going was enough to cover up the sound of Neil's movements.

The percolator fizzled behind her and she let out a soft sigh. She wished they could be more open about their relationship. Keeping it a secret from their daughter was getting tougher, even though it was in their girl's best interest. Kelsey knew Rikki would be overcome with joy once she knew about it, and would be heartbroken if things didn't work out.

She cricked her neck and winced as she heard the door between her bedroom and the bathroom click. It sounded so darn loud.

Rikki slowly walked in with an armload of clothes and her face stony. "Where were you last night?"

Kelsey's eyebrows shot upwards at Rikki's tone. "I was home. Why?"

Her daughter's eyes narrowed into thin slits and her lips compressed. "You're lying."

The accusation felt like bullets to Kelsey.

She stared at her daughter incredulously. "What?"

"I don't believe you!" Rikki snapped and her lower lip started to tremble.

"Why not?" Kelsey asked and cocked her head.

With a glare, the girl defiantly dropped the clothing in her arms to expose a pair of men's boxers.

Kelsey's stomach dropped to her toes when she recognized them as Neil's, a pair that had been in her basket of folded laundry by the hall archway.

"You're seeing someone?" Rikki yelled and held the underwear in her mother's face. Tears started to stream down her cheeks, her face turned red and her teeth clenched together in fury.

Kelsey winced. "Rikki, it's not what it looks like—"

"Yes, it is!" the girl screamed.

"No, it isn't." She reached out and tried to touch her daughter's hair, but the girl hopped backwards. "Rikki—"

"How could you? You know I want you and Dad to get together so we can be a real family." Rikki started to back toward the entryway.

"It's not what you think," Kelsey replied and took a step toward her daughter.

"Yes, it is. You're having sex with someone else while—" Her words were cut off by a loud sob as she threw the boxers at the cupboards.

Kelsey managed to get closer to her. "If you will just calm down and listen to me–"

"I don't have to listen to you. You're not my real mom. My real mom is dead!" the girl screamed painfully and started to cry harder.

Kelsey's heart ripped wide open at her daughter's words. "Yes, I am your mother. I love you."

Rikki glared at her and shook her head slowly. "That doesn't make a mother. You gave me up."

"I wanted you to have a better life. Rikki, calm down and

listen to me, please." Kelsey tried to touch her shoulder.

Rikki shook it off. "Don't touch me!"

Kelsey's hands shot upwards. "I won't touch you. Just take a deep breath and listen to me."

"I don't want to hear your lies," Rikki shrieked. "Leave me alone!" She turned and ran toward the front door.

Kelsey's heart sank further, which prompted her feet in to motion. She managed to dive for the door a nanosecond before Rikki and blocked the girl's exit.

"Let me out," the girl cried.

Kelsey stood firm, spread her arms flat against the walls and panted as she pressed her back against the cold metal door. "I'm not letting you go outside like this, Rikki. Calm down and think of what you're doing before you do something you'll regret." She kept her voice level and quiet.

"Sorry? The only thing I'm sorry about is finding out my mother is a whore."

Ouch. Thanks for the final blow, Rikki.

Kelsey felt her cheeks turn icy, and her knees started to give out. She locked them, and although she tried to keep her expression serious, tears burned her eyes and her throat closed at the insult. "I'm not a whore," she said softly.

The girl's face turned red in fury. "You're always spending time with my dad, making me think we're going to be a family, and you're screwing someone else. Only whores do that."

"Erika Lynn, that's enough." The firm, male command echoed in the entryway.

Rikki froze, her face pale and her eyes wide. Slowly, she turned her head, and her face turned green when she met her dad's gaze. Her hands dropped to her sides and she cringed under his scrutiny.

Kelsey recognized the look on Neil's face, a combination of fury, shock and sadness. She absently hugged herself.

Neil folded his arms across his chest and glowered at their daughter. "What in the hell do you think you're doing?"

Rikki's shoulders slumped guiltily. "I was—"

"Hurting your mother? Erika Lynn Falcon, you know we do not insult each other," he scolded angrily and took a step in her direction.

Rikki cringed. "Yes, sir," she mumbled.

"Apologize to your mother."

With her head hanged in humiliation, Rikki stared at her sneakers and mumbled, "Sorry."

Kelsey nodded and exchanged an embarrassed and sorrowful glance with Neil.

He moved his gaze back to Rikki and in a much calmer voice instructed, "Go clean up your mess and sit in the living room while your mother and I talk about an appropriate punishment."

Rikki nodded and shoved her hands into her jeans pockets as she started to walk by her father with a downcast look.

He held out a hand and said, "Give me your phone."

She pulled it out of her pocket and gave it to him with a roll of her eyes before she skulked into the kitchen.

When she was out of sight, Neil's shoulders drooped. "Dammit," he muttered with a sigh.

"Yeah, busted," Kelsey replied and sniffled softly.

He shoved the phone into his pocket and moved to stand beside her. He put his hand on her cheek. "Are you okay? She didn't hurt you, did she?"

Kelsey shook her head and leaned into the caress. "I'm fine. I'm shocked and sad at her actions." She glanced toward the living room mournfully and back at him. "I know she's wanted us to get together for a long time, but I didn't realize how much until now."

"It's no excuse for her to call you names," Neil whispered and slid his arm around her shoulders. "She knows better than that."

Her head fell to his shoulder. "I think being called a whore by my own daughter hurt more than anything. Well, other than being told I wasn't her real mom."

"She's damn lucky I don't believe in corporal punishment, because I'd be spanking her so hard, she wouldn't sit down for a month."

"We'll figure out something that she won't forget," she murmured and snuggled closer to his side. "How long do you think she should go without her phone?"

"At least a month should do it."

"No visits with Taffy for how long?"

"I'm not sure," he murmured distractedly. "I'll think about it while you're getting dressed. I can't seem to think about anything other than you when I know you're wearing nothing under that robe." His gaze flicked to the bottom of the V, where the valley between her breasts was visible.

"There's always later, after she goes to bed."

Neil inhaled sharply and gently pushed her away. "Damn you, woman, go get dressed before I go nuts," he muttered.

Kelsey stuck her tongue out at him before she sauntered away, with a deliberate swing of her hips, and giggled when she heard him mutter an insult about the two girls in his life in jest.

An hour later, Kelsey and Neil doled out the punishment.

Rikki's eyes rolled. "How am I going to live without my phone for that long?"

"You'll survive. Your mother and I grew up without that kind of thing, and we managed just fine," Neil stated.

"Yeah, but for a whole month? It's not like I hit Kelsey." Rikki pouted and crossed her arms across her chest.

Kelsey sighed. *She didn't hit me with her fists, but she still cut me with her words.*

"You know we don't call each other names in this house," he scolded. "Also, you're not allowed to use the computer unless it's for a school project for that month."

"Dad!" Rikki whined.

"We could make it two months," Kelsey threatened.

"Or three," Neil said with a stern look at their daughter.

Rikki glared at them and slumped in her chair.

"No sleepovers either, and no visiting Taffy or any other friends. You're grounded," Kelsey said. "You're going to come here or to your dad's straight from school, do your homework, do your chores and watch TV until bedtime."

Rikki's lower lip stuck out and started to tremble. "I'm being put in jail."

"You should have thought of that before you called your mother a whore," Neil snarled.

"I thought she was having sex with some jerk."

"My sex life is none of your business," Kelsey muttered.

"It is if you're seeing some asshole that doesn't like me!"

"Erika Lynn, be quiet, or you'll be in deeper trouble," Neil snapped.

Rikki turned her glower back to him and shut up.

She has a point. What if I had been sleeping with someone she didn't know, and who didn't want a child, especially a teenager? Kelsey filed it away to discuss with Neil at a later date and refocused on the latest upset.

Rikki started to mutter a swear word under her breath. "Yes, sir," she mumbled.

"You let your mother and I know where you are at all times. No sneaking off with Taffy or someone else, unless you want more trouble on your head."

Rikki nodded with an exaggerated roll of her eyes.

"Go finish your homework," he ordered.

Rikki didn't move. "One question."

"What?" Kelsey asked warily.

"When did you two start dating?"

Neil and Kelsey exchanged a long glance.

Kelsey felt the blood rise to her cheeks.

Neil cricked his neck uncomfortably.

"It's been a few weeks," Kelsey mumbled.

Rikki peered at them. "Uh huh."

Neil muttered, "You were in the Valley with your class-mates when things started."

Rikki blinked. "The weekend of our class trip to Ste. Anne?"

"Yep," Kelsey admitted reluctantly.

"I knew you liked Kelsey, Dad, but I didn't really think you two were together."

"It's not like we haven't been dropping hints," Kelsey mumbled. "Some of those late nights weren't spent at the computer."

Rikki's wide gaze landed on her. "You mean, each time you spent the night at our house, you two weren't really editing, you were—" Her face turned a little green and she grimaced. "Gross! Too much information," she gagged.

"Yeah, your parents are having sex. Get used to it," Neil muttered.

Kelsey kicked his shin under the table. "Let's leave it at we're dating and seeing how it goes."

"What's going to happen to me if you two break up?"

"We'll work together for your sake," Neil promised. "Kelsey is one of your legal guardians, so we'll still be consulting on punishments and everything else, even if it happens."

The girl nodded.

"Go do your homework while your dad and I work on his next article," Kelsey prompted. At her daughter's grimace, she added with a sigh, "For real. We'll even keep the bedroom door open so you can see we're not doing anything other than working."

Rikki nodded and left the kitchen.

That night, Neil and Rikki went back to his house so Rikki

could adapt to the idea of her parents being a couple without her mother around. He wasn't pleased when Kelsey suggested it on the sly, and only agreed to it when she explained that having her around might not be a good idea if Rikki wanted to talk to him about it alone.

Rikki was at her desk when Neil knocked on the door and peeked in.

She didn't look up. "What?"

He leaned against the doorjamb. "I thought you'd want to talk to me without Kelsey around."

She shrugged. "I'm busy."

He stared at her for a moment and sighed. "Okay, forget it." He straightened and turned.

"Dad?"

He stopped. "Yeah?"

"This project isn't due for a few days. I can finish it later, if you want to talk," she mumbled.

He nodded and sat down on her bed.

Rikki turned her desk chair to face him and they stared at each other for a few minutes.

Neil leaned forward to rest his elbows on his thighs and linked his fingers together. "I owe you an apology."

"For what?"

He let out a long sigh and glanced around the room before he met his daughter's gaze. "I should have warned you that Kelsey and I were—you know." He shifted uncomfortably.

"Fucking?" she said sarcastically.

He averted his gaze and felt his cheeks flame.

"That's what you were doing, right? Having sex?"

"Rikki, there's more to it than sex." Neil cleared his throat and cricked his neck.

She rolled her eyes and muttered, "I know."

"I still owe you an apology for allowing you to find out like that."

She shrugged. "I'm glad it's you, and not some jerk who hates me."

"If things had gone differently, Kelsey and I might have wound up together years ago."

She stared at him. "If you two liked each other back then, why didn't it happen?"

He let out a long breath and moved his gaze to his hands. "Things were a lot different. You know how abusive her mother was, and why she couldn't keep you."

Rikki nodded. "She was scared her mother would hurt me."

He raised his gaze to hers. "Or that she herself would do the same thing to you."

"Kelsey wouldn't do that. She bitches about Punky all of the time, but she's never hurt him. She loves him, and she loves cats."

"And your point is?"

"Anyone who laughed when they were covered in mud thanks to chowder head would never hurt a kid," Rikki said smugly.

Neil grinned. *Smart girl.* "Good point." He stood up. "I'll let you get back to it."

"Dad, do you think you and Kelsey will get married?"

So, it's starting. He shrugged. "We really haven't talked about it yet. Why?"

"Just wondering."

He reached out and ruffled her hair. "I wouldn't mind marrying Kelsey, but only if you're okay with it. Otherwise, we'll keep things as is, or I'll stop seeing her."

He was almost out the door when Rikki said, "I'm okay with it."

A slow grin formed across his face.

After Rikki went to bed, Neil went into his office and shut

the door. He sat down behind his desk, pulled a memory stick out of his pocket, and stared at it. On it was a copy of the file containing Kelsey's story, in its rough draft, that he had gotten that morning when Kelsey was trying to get Rikki out of the house.

The story wasn't finished yet, but apparently Rhonda Johnson didn't care.

She only cared about making money. If that meant exploiting others and wrecking relationships, so be it.

Same with ruining others' security and income.

Did he want to be financially secure for a year and lose Kelsey forever?

Or did he want to be happy for life with Kelsey, but lose everything that his daughter needed, like food, a house, and everything else?

He flipped it around his fingers a few times and let out a long sigh.

I wish there was a way I could keep Kelsey and be financially secure, but I can't find it.

Shit.

He straightened in his chair, flattened his lips together and let out a long, tired sigh.

The memory stick slid into its slot a second later.

It was copied, uploaded and sent off in an email less than a minute later.

He sat there, staring at his monitor for a few long minutes before it sank in what happened.

Nausea hit him like a truck, his vision blurred, and his hands began to shake.

Oh, shit. What the hell have I done?

He covered his face with his hands and let out a low, long moan of agony.

I'm so sorry, Kelsey. Forgive me, sweetheart.

Chapter Twelve

Things went back to normal after that. The only change was that Kelsey spent the night with Neil instead of in her daughter's room on the days they were working. Rikki grimaced a few times after seeing her mom exit her dad's room when Kelsey didn't get up before her daughter, but soon adjusted to it.

During Kelsey's time off, she and the cats were at Neil's house more than hers. There were some weeks they didn't go home at all, other than to stock up on cat food or bring more of her clothing over to Neil's house.

Easter brought the hope of spring. It was a fun long weekend, even with Kelsey working.

That Tuesday, Neil was offered a one-year contract for the magazine. He stared at it incredulously and nausea bubbled up in his throat as he recalled why Rhonda had offered him such a lucrative deal. He hadn't gotten around to telling Kelsey about sending the woman the first chapter of her story yet, and hoped that they wouldn't call her before he could work up the courage to tell her.

Kelsey immediately told him to accept it after he picked her up from work that day.

"If you take it, it'll look good on your resume, and another, better magazine may come along after this one runs out," she explained and reached over to put a hand on his thigh. "It'll be a full year of security for both of you."

"She's a bitch, Kelsey, one of the worst to work for in the entire business."

"She's been really good with you lately; don't you think that means something?"

His hands tightened around the steering wheel. *You won't think that once you find out I had to sell my soul to get it.* "She's probably desperate for someone who will work for beans, and I'm it. She knows how little work is out there for freelancers like me right now," he muttered.

Kelsey stared at him blankly. "She knows you're one of the best out there and is scared someone else is going to snap you up."

If only you knew. He forced the nausea away and cricked his neck. "I'm only as good as my editor. She's been good to me lately only because you've been helping me get things so perfect she doesn't have to do a damn thing with them."

"Bullshit. You're good, Neil, and she knows it. Just sign the damn thing, for Christ's sake."

With a shake of his head and bile rising in his throat again, he mumbled, "I'll think about it."

One week later

"Kelsey? This is Jaiden Lefebvre." She rattled off the name of the magazine she worked for, and her position on its staff.

Kelsey didn't recognize the woman's name, but knew the magazine whose owner was driving Neil crazy with her constant red marks on his articles.

She wondered why this editor was calling her. She didn't work for them, Neil did.

The voice on the airways was gentle and sweet. "I'm calling to ask you if you would be interested in working with us, as a writer. I've been assigned to be your editor, if you come aboard."

"A writer?" Kelsey asked, dumbfounded.

"We'd like you to be our first featured author in our new

column," Jaiden replied and explained what the company was doing.

Kelsey listened to the woman ramble on about making their magazine more marketable to teenagers with half an ear while her mind skittered from question to question.

How did this woman know I'm writing a story, and how does she know what it's about?

Kelsey asked, "I'm sorry, but how did you get my name, and a sample of my work? I didn't send anything to you."

"Mr. Falcon sent us a copy of its first chapter a few weeks ago, after my boss drove him crazy wanting to know the name of his editor, and what you did for a living." Her voice faded.

Neil had showed her work to someone without her permission? Why would he do such a thing, when he knew she wasn't ready and didn't think she could cut it and get published?

The questions continued to churn in her mind as Jaiden's voice came back into focus. "I really loved the character of Moshomi. She's brilliant, funny, sweet and kind!"

Kelsey's stomach churned and a headache started to form between her eyes as she listened to the editor ramble on about her work. She hoped she made the appropriate noises at the right time.

"I'll be emailing a copy of the contract for you to go over later today. Take a few days to think about it, and talk it over with Mr. Falcon, if you want. He's worked with us on and off for a long time, so he can give you the ins and outs of how we work."

"Yes, that sounds fine," Kelsey mumbled distantly.

"I'll call you in a few days if I haven't heard back from you. Welcome to the team, Kelsey."

Kelsey hit *off* on her phone and her hand slowly lowered to her side as the knowledge that Neil had betrayed her trust started to hit her.

How dare he? He knew she didn't like people other than him and Rikki touching her writing, and she wasn't ready to send anything out yet. Her story wasn't finished, or edited properly, and probably would have never been sent out if he hadn't gone behind her back, stolen a copy of it and sent it off to that high-handed bitch.

Her knees gave out, and she sank into a chair, sobbing, as she recalled the contract offer.

Neil handed me to the wolves to advance his career.

The sound of his office door slamming open shot through the house like an explosion.

Neil whipped around to give Rikki a firm reminder about not disturbing him. He was startled to see Kelsey standing in the doorway, her hands on her hips, her eyes narrowed and spitting sparks, and her entire body tense in fury.

"You low-down, dirty, rotten prick! How dare you?" she hissed with clenched teeth.

He backed up a step and his stomach started to churn nervously. "What did I do?"

"Like you don't know? How convenient you'd forget stabbing me in the back when there's a lot of money shoved in your face," she bellowed.

Neil's eyes closed and he felt his face turn cold.

Damn that Rhonda for painting me into a corner.

Nausea shot up his throat when he opened his eyes and met her accusing stare.

And damn me for going behind Kelsey's back.

He averted his gaze and lowered his head. His shoulders slumped. He had broken the trust of the woman he loved, all to protect their daughter and his career. Once Kelsey's faith in someone was broken, there was no going back. She'd always immediately cut off the person and walked away for good, to protect herself from future harm.

He'd be lucky to talk to her via email after what he'd done

to her, and he deserved it, too.

"What? Don't you have anything to say for yourself?" she demanded around a sob.

He shook his head and tried not to show her how much he was hurting.

She stared at him silently for a moment and held her hands up. "Fine. I guess that's my cue to get my stuff and get out of here," she choked out and turned to walk away.

His gaze flew upwards as he heard her foot hit the floor. It was like the sound of a gong just before the executioner delivered the death blow. He couldn't let her walk away without hearing his explanation, and there was no way he was going to let go of her over something that had been out of his control.

He needed her in his life—she was as vital to him as breathing, and he had to prove to her just how much she meant to him, somehow.

"Kelsey, wait!" he yelled at her retreating back.

"Fuck off." She ran into his bedroom and dove into the closet.

He ran after her and yanked a hanger out of her hands. "Calm down and listen to me for a second."

She grabbed another hanger off the rail and tried to push him away when he reached for it. "Why, so you can do it again? No way in hell."

He tossed the one in his hands aside and grabbed her around the waist from behind to pull her away from the clothing. Her feet lifted from the floor as she fought to get loose.

Neil grimaced as her nails painfully ripped layers of skin off his forearm.

"Kelsey, stop, please," he hissed in her ear as she kicked and wriggled around. "I didn't want to do it, but it was either give it to her or never work in the industry again. She wouldn't take no for an answer and—"

"I don't care," Kelsey cried and struggled to get free. "You know not to go behind my back and do something like this. I trusted you more than anyone else in the world, and you did it anyway."

"I shouldn't have done it. I wouldn't have if she hadn't put my back against the wall and threatened me," Neil said painfully as the agony of his actions hit him full force. "Kelsey, sweetheart, I'm so sorry for hurting you."

Tears flowed down her face, her face contoured in agony, and her eyes closed as her body sagged in defeat. Sobs shook her frame, her head fell backwards to rest on his shoulder, and her legs started to give way.

Neil eased her to the floor and held on to her as he started to cry too.

"You didn't just break my trust, you broke my heart," she gasped after a minute.

"I know, and I'm so, so sorry, baby," he choked out and pressed his face against her neck.

"Why did you do it? You could have told her to shove her head up her ass and you'd find someone better to work for! She's a low-down bitch, and you hate working for her."

Moment of truth. "Maybe I did it because deep down, I want to see the woman I'm in love with reach her dreams too."

Kelsey pushed his head from hers. She looked over her shoulder to stare at him incredulously with her mouth agape. "Uh, what did you just say?"

"You heard me," he mumbled and didn't meet her gaze.

"Did you just tell me you're—?"

He nodded and started brushing tears off her face with his thumb. "It wasn't about money, Kelsey. Rhonda made threats, and good ones, but not good enough to make me stab you in the back so I could get ahead," he whispered. "I did it to give you the push you needed. I remembered your dream to be published someday."

She nodded. "But not by having the one person I trust most go behind my back to see it happen, or so they could move up in the world." Her eyes slid shut and she leaned her temple into his cheek as her tears started to flow again.

He started rocking her back and forth and tightened his arm around her waist. "I know," he whispered, and kissed the side of her head. "I convinced myself you'd be too happy to be upset with me when you found out."

She trembled in agony and shook her head. "You betrayed me, even if you thought it was best for me," she choked out.

"It makes me sick to know that I did that to you, sweetheart," he replied. "Can you forgive me for being such a stupid asshole?"

She shrugged. "It wasn't all in my best interest. It was either do it, or never work as a freelancer again. It was greed that did it, not wanting to see me get published."

Misery shot through Neil's body and his teeth clenched together. He had to prove to her that it wasn't about the money, and he knew how to do it.

He eased away from her and rose to his feet. Kelsey leaned forward with her arms wrapped around her stomach and her head hung in grief as her sobs shook her body.

He ran out of the closet and bedroom, across the hallway into his office, and quickly scanned the room for what he wanted.

It was on the corner of his desk. He grabbed it, removed its contents and tossed the folder over his shoulder as he ran back into his room, and the closet.

Kelsey was still sitting as he left her and glared at him when he knelt beside her and held the stack of papers in front of her. He flipped to the last page, to show her the empty signature line.

"Are you going to twist the knife by signing it in front of me?"

"Nope."

Neil ripped the contract in half.

She stared at him with wide eyes. "What in the hell are you doing?" she demanded. "I thought that meant a year of security for you and our daughter."

He snarled and tore it in half again. "I'd rather never work again than lose you over something so damn stupid!" he said and kept repeating his actions until he had a pile of small pieces of paper.

"You're an idiot for not taking it."

"I'm an idiot for letting that bitch think she owned the world. If this is what it takes to prove to you how much I love you, so be it!"

He tossed the paper into the air. It rained upon them like ragged pieces of confetti, landing in her hair and his and strewn across the floor of the closet.

Kelsey caught one in her hand as it flittered toward the floor. She slapped her other hand over her mouth and coughed in surprise. "I can't believe you just did that."

Neil stared at the mess he'd created. "Uh, neither can I," he mumbled, dumbfounded.

Her gaze rose to meet his, and they stared at each other.

"I'm really sorry I went behind your back, sweetheart. Will you forgive me?"

Her eyes flooded with tears as she nodded.

Neil flopped down on the floor beside her, pulled her into his arms to hug her and kissed her hard. A shot of jubilation went up his spine when she snuggled closer to him and responded.

"Now what are you going to do?" Kelsey asked a few minutes later.

He snorted. "I'll figure it out. Rhonda Johnson isn't the end all and be all of the magazines out there, even if she thinks she owns the world."

She reached up to cup his cheek. "We'll figure it out, together."

A smile slowly started to form on his face. "Together. You're not going anywhere?"

She shook her head and kissed him. "I'm staying right here, and not just for Rikki's sake, but for ours. I love you too much to walk away."

"You're in love with me?" he asked. His smile became a grin and joy replaced guilt and sorrow.

She averted her gaze and nodded shyly.

He kissed her again. "That's the best thing I've heard all day."

They settled into the corner, with the bits of paper strewn around them and tears drying on Kelsey's cheeks. She glanced around at the papers and shook her head. "I still can't believe you did that. When do you want to go check job listings for freelancers?"

"I don't have to," he replied and smiled smugly. "I got a call from an editor at another magazine just before you barged in here and started yelling at me."

"Does he want to take you on for an article or two?"

Neil shook his head. "He wants me to sign a three-year exclusive deal with them, and I think I'm going to do it. It doesn't pay as much a year as the one with—Oomph!"

Whatever he was going to say next was cut off and forgotten as Kelsey threw her arms around his neck and kissed him.

"Dad? Are you working?"

Neil opened his eyes and lifted his head. Was it late afternoon already? "Back here!"

Her footsteps approached the bedroom. "Do you know where Kelsey is? I went to her house, and it was only Punky and the cats—"

"I'm here," Kelsey called out softly, her voice husky.

Their daughter's footsteps stopped abruptly. "Uh, okay. I'll be in my room."

Neil sighed and exchanged an eye roll with Kelsey. "We're decent, I promise."

Her footsteps became louder as she entered his bedroom. "Where are you guys?"

"In here," Kelsey replied.

Rikki popped her head around the doorjamb and pulled back. "What are you two doing in here? I hope this isn't your idea of kinky!" She gagged from around the corner.

"It's safe," Neil muttered, "and no, it's nothing kinky."

Rikki slowly peeked around the corner. Her grin faded into a nose wrinkle when she beheld them sitting against the back wall of the closet with their arms around each other and the pieces of torn paper in their hair, on their clothing, and scattered across the carpet. "What are you two doing?"

"Deciding our future," Neil replied.

Rikki stared at them oddly. "In the closet?"

"Why not?" Kelsey asked.

"I'll never understand you two," she muttered and walked away with a flip of her hair.

Behind her retreating back, her parents shared a snicker.

"I'm going to turn down the offer. I don't want to work for anyone who would sink to such shitty methods out of greed," Kelsey said after they got into bed that night.

"Are you sure about this, Kelsey? I don't want you passing up on something because you're pissed off at someone at their company." Neil's arm slid around her waist.

She put her hand on his chest and nodded. "I can't overlook the fact she used you and your lack of work to stab me with her knife, just to get what she wanted. If I worked with her company at all, I'd feel like I'm selling all of us into slavery, and I don't want that."

Neil shrugged. "I'm behind you, either way."

She smiled and kissed him. "How did the talk with that other editor go?"

"He's excited, and keeps going on about how much he's wanted me to join the team for a while, but their timing never seemed to line up when I was available," he replied with a grin. "I managed to haggle a little extra out of him as a signing bonus."

"Yes!" Kelsey cheered softly and pumped a fist in the air. "No more Rhonda Johnson for either of us. She can kiss Punky's ass. Or would it be more appropriate for him to eat her favourite designer purse?"

"Only if he pukes it up all over her desk and shits in her custom-made shoes as a bonus," Neil added with a snicker.

"Ah, the ultimate corgi revenge. I'd love to see him give it to her instead of us for a change," she giggled.

"Me too," Neil said and kissed her.

"I understand, Ms. Wagner, but—"

"Miss Lefebvre, it's not your fault, it's your boss'. You're a good reader, from what I've heard, and if you weren't working for that snob, I'd gladly work with you," Kelsey said.

"Thank you, but you didn't hear what I said," Jaiden Lefebvre mumbled.

"What did you say?"

"I showed your work to a friend of mine that works for a big publishing house."

Kelsey's eyes widened and fury started to rise in her gut. "How dare you do that? Neil submitted it to you without my permission, and now you're passing it around like it's your work? I ought to sue your asses off for trying to steal it and breaking copyrights," she snarled.

"Ms. Wagner, I am not trying to break copyrights or steal

your work," Jaiden whimpered.

"Then why are you showing it to others without my written permission?" Kelsey snapped.

"I thought it was too good to put into the magazine. Ms. Johnson doesn't deserve to have something that high quality. This magazine is garbage, and she knows it, so she's willing to do whatever it takes to make it look better," the young editor mumbled.

Kelsey's initial burst of anger weakened. "It sounds like you hate it there as much as Neil did," she said softly.

Jaiden sighed. "Yes, I do, but you don't know that. I think your work could make a splash in the market, but as a book, or a series."

"Really?"

"Yes, I do. I've been offered a job with this other guy, and I'm taking it. The best of it is, he said if you want to talk about a contract, we can in few weeks. He also said I can be your editor and go-to person there."

Kelsey's eyes widened and a slow grin started spreading across her face. "I don't know what to say."

"How's about I call you next week to set up a meeting? That should be enough time to think about it and talk it over with Mr. Falcon."

"Yeah, that would be wonderful, thank you."

"No, thank *you*, Ms. Wagner. I can't wait to start working with you, in a real publishing house, not some rinky-dink crap-hole," Jaiden chirped, relief flooding her voice. "We'll talk soon."

"Okay," Kelsey replied distantly and hung up the phone.

She jumped when Neil demanded from behind her, "Did that old bitch try to force you to sign on with them or something?"

She slowly turned to face him with wide eyes and a shake of her head. "No, she didn't."

"Then what happened?"

"Miss Lefebvre is leaving the magazine and going to a publishing house." Kelsey set down the phone and shook her head to clear the cobwebs as she flopped down on the couch.

"So? You didn't sign on with the magazine, did you?"

"No, I wouldn't be that stupid." She lifted her head and stared up at him. "Miss Lefebvre showed my work to her new boss, and he loved it so much he wants to talk about a book deal," she whispered distantly.

Neil stared at her dumbfounded, and as it sank in, a grin slowly spread across his face. "You're serious? Her friend is really going to offer you a book deal?"

Kelsey shook her head. "I can't believe it either." Her eyes widened and she slapped a hand over her mouth as a mad giggle erupted out of her chest. "I'm going to be an author. Holy shit!"

CHAPTER THIRTEEN

Neil started working full time for his new employer later that month. It was a small but reputable parenting magazine located in Charlottetown, Prince Edward Island. Although the work was more intense than it had been with the other magazine, he liked it better. He didn't have as many deadlines or last-minute changes looming over his head and seemed more relaxed with his new job. Kelsey still helped him with his editing, although that improved over time.

Kelsey was still working at the gas station part-time. On her days off, she worked on her story, and was over at Neil and Rikki's house a lot.

In May, she finally met Jaiden Lefebvre for the first time, and liked the young woman on sight. Jaiden's twinkling blue eyes and high excitement were irresistible, as was her enthusiasm for her new workplace. The publishing house was located in Chester, in an old house that felt like it should have been part of a story. Kelsey's mind started flipping ideas around.

Maybe there's at least one story I can get from this beautiful old place, she thought, caressing the edge of a doorjamb. *Another day. Today is about Moshomi and her journey.*

She turned her attention back to the young editor in front of her.

Jaiden's hands never seemed to stop moving as she explained the contract to Kelsey and Neil in detail. "So, what do you think? If it's not enough, I can talk to Ryan about a bigger percentage, or a larger signing bonus."

Kelsey blinked at the amount shown and shook her head. It was astronomical in her opinion. "Isn't this too much for an unknown?" she sputtered, flabbergasted.

"Not here. Ryan believes in keeping everyone happy — he's very author orientated. They're the ones who keep up his great reputation, after all," Jaiden chirped with a wink.

"I'm — gee whiz. I feel like I'm — Neil, what do you think?" She turned and stared up at him.

"Whatever you want to do, Kelsey. I'm with you all the way."

"Don't you think it's — "

"Just take it, or I'll sic Rikki and chowder head on you," he threatened.

She shot him a filthy look before she stared at the contract again and let out a long breath. She picked up the pen, held it over the dotted line, then with a look of determination, signed her name.

Jaiden shook her limp hand enthusiastically. "Welcome to the team, Ms. Wagner!"

Kelsey nodded absently and whispered, "Did I just do what I think I just did?"

"Yeah, you did," Neil replied as Jaiden walked out of the office to alert her boss.

"Holy shit."

He snickered and looped an arm around her waist. "Nope, holy best seller list."

"You wish." She leaned into his side. "Oh my god, I'm going to be an author."

Neil tightened his arm. "Wrong, you *are* an author. Congrats, Kelsey, you made it."

She gave him a watery grin and threw her arms around his neck in excitement.

Spring exploded with warmer weather, high humidity and a burst of leaves and flowers. Life was hectic, and although it wasn't easy, they settled into a routine that consisted of Kelsey being at Neil's house more than she was at hers.

They discussed moving in together, but decided it could wait until the lease on Kelsey's house was finished that fall. They would be paying rent on it anyway, so her main residence was kept as is, even though she and the cats were not there a lot. It was a slow, easy time, and they grew closer and happier by the day as their courtship blossomed.

Despite his happiness, Neil realized something wasn't right, and couldn't figure out why.

It was in the middle of June when he realized the final bond wasn't there. He and Kelsey were a couple, and even though he was loved having her with him and their daughter a lot of the time, wanted it to become permanent.

They were editing his latest article the following week when he asked, "Kelsey, are you happy?"

She blinked and shrugged. "I wouldn't be here if I wasn't." She stared up at him quizzically. "What brought that on?" She turned back to the stack of papers and drew a line through a paragraph.

Neil's eyes rolled and he gently took the pencil out of her hand. "I've been thinking."

When she started to stiffen, he quickly added, "Before you think the worst, I'm not saying I want to slow things down. We'll be a complete family in a couple of months, and I really want you to move in with us in the fall."

"Why did you ask me if I was happy? Did I do or say something to make you think otherwise?" She reached out and covered his hand with hers.

He squeezed her fingers. "No, you didn't. This is the happiest I've seen you. I just had a silly idea in my head, and — oh, forget it." He moved his hands away from hers and turned back to the computer.

"I've never been happier than I am now. Being with you and Rikki, and knowing I'll be moving in with you both soon, is like a dream come true." She touched his jaw with her fingers and whispered, "What silly idea are you talking about?"

He rolled his shoulders nervously. "I was thinking about making this," he pointed to her and the rest of the house, "permanent, once you're settled in."

Her brow furrowed in puzzlement. "Huh?"

He let out a long breath and without looking at her, mumbled, "I'm talking about us getting married, either before you move in, or sometime next year."

Looking shocked, she stared at him silently for so long that he wondered if asking her was a mistake. He cringed as she blinked at him.

"I—whoa," she finally whispered. "Are you serious?"

He leaned over and gave her a long, tender kiss that had her trembling and breathless by the time he lifted his head. "I am, and the sooner the better."

Her eyes were still glazed in shock and her grin was goofy when she asked, "Why now? We've been together only for a couple of months. Shouldn't we wait a while before we take that step?"

He shook his head and smiled. "I've been in love with you for a long time. I don't want to wait any longer to have you as my wife."

"It's not because I'm Rikki's mom, is it?" she asked warily.

"No," he whispered reassuringly and kissed her. "I fell in love with you the first night you cried on my shoulder at the shelter, and never got over you."

"I see." She pulled back and stiffened, a signal her internal walls were going up. "If that's the case, why didn't you say or do something back then?"

"I-I don't know what you mean."

Her glare shot sparks of anger at him. "If you were really in love with me as you claim, why didn't you tell me, or show me?" she demanded. "It wasn't like I was hiding my feelings for you."

He blinked at the ferocity emanating from her. Remorse kicked his gut when he remembered how happy she had been to see him during the first year after they had met, and the grief in her eyes when he introduced her to Rita.

Shit.

"Kelsey, I was a counselor there, and I would have taken advantage of you—"

"You weren't my counselor after I moved out." She leapt up from the chair and started pacing the room. Her hands fisted by her sides, and her entire body shook. She started to cry.

Aw fuck, me and my big yap. Why did I tell her that?

Neil jumped out of his chair and tried to pull her into his arms.

She backed up a step.

Bile rose in his throat. "Kelsey, stop and listen to me."

"I fell in love with you back then, and you didn't do anything to discourage it, Neil. You let it happen. Instead of putting some distance between us, you kept coming around and talking to me. You should have left it alone and walked away. You're such an arrogant prick!" she cried. She fisted her hands in her hair and sobs shook her frame.

He put his hands on her upper arms.

She shook them off.

He frantically whispered, "I didn't want for it to happen, and I'm sorry I hurt you. I was scared I'd ruin your life if we got together. You had just come out of a rotten situation. You needed a friend, not a lover, and as much as I wanted to be that special guy for you, I couldn't do it."

She screamed, "We could have been together then if you had stopped making excuses. All of those years, wasted, because you were too fucking scared to do anything about it!"

"I wasn't scared. I was watching out for you, because I love you and wanted what was best for you," he bellowed the denial, and felt sick when his gut kicked the truth.

He had been frightened, of her and the feelings she provoked in him, and of how much she had meant to him. He had been worried she had fallen for him because he was kind to her.

I held back because I was terrified of losing her.

He felt sick as she raised her glare to his pleading gaze and he could see all of his fears, pain and sorrow reflected back at him, along with an underlying determination and the slamming of internal doors.

Despite everything, his deepest and innermost terror had become a reality.

Fuck. I've lost her for good.

She shook her head, held up her hands, turned and quietly walked out of the room.

A moment later, the click of the back door and the sound of her car starting echoed loudly in the silent house.

Neil sank to the floor, curled up in a fetal position, and held his stomach as his sobs started.

Two days later

Each breath he took was a reminder of Kelsey's last words to him, and their quarrel kept repeating itself in his mind.

Neil clamped the pillow over his head and growled in misery as he heard Kelsey's accusations run through his head again.

He leapt from the bed and ran into the bathroom, when the nausea overtook him. His empty stomach only produced dry heaves that shot agony through his ribcage and spine.

He slumped to the floor in a heap beside the toilet and put his forearm across his eyes.

Why had he opened his big mouth and told her he had fallen in love with her back then? If he had kept his counsel, things would be different.

Another wave of queasiness shook his weakened body, and the banging on his bedroom door, followed by a loud bark and whine, went ignored as her words crashed through his mind over and over again.

Kill me. Just do it now and get it over with, instead of torturing me.

A bang penetrated his mind this time, and when he heard a muffled, distantly familiar voice calling his name, he clamped his hands over his ears, squeezed his eyes shut, and ground his teeth together.

"Neil, open up damn you!"

He rolled onto his side and pressed his face against the icy porcelain of the toilet's base.

The thumping stopped.

Neil shivered, curled up into a fetal position, and let out a groan as his teeth started to chatter.

"Jesus Christ, what the hell do you think you're doing?"

A hand grabbed his arm.

He pushed it away.

"Oh, no you don't."

He distantly recognized the voice as Ruby's.

He cringed. The only way she would have come over was if Rikki had alerted her and Gina. One didn't argue with either of them, but out of the two, Ruby was the most determined, and scariest when she was on a roll.

Shit on a stick. She must have busted the lock to get in here.

He unsuccessfully tried to shove her away again.

Something wet hit his face, hard.

He shook his head to fling water out of his eyes and glared at her. "Leave me alone, Ruby."

She mirrored it with a scoff. "Why, so you can die of dehydration or starve yourself to death?"

He turned his face away from hers and muttered, "Get out."

"I don't give two shits if you want to commit suicide, but isn't this taking things to the extreme? It takes at least three days to die of dehydration, and even longer if you starve yourself. I thought if you tried it, it would be quick, fast, easy, and wouldn't put the rest of us through the horror of watching you die like this."

He clamped his hands over his ears and squeezed his eyes shut.

She toed him in the leg. "Fine with me. I don't give a shit if you die or not, but think of Rikki."

Rikki?

Neil's eyes popped open. "What about her?"

"She doesn't deserve to lose another parent. She's already lost her adoptive parents, and god knows where her birth mom is right now. Don't you think she deserves more than losing you too?"

Neil blinked.

"She's lost, confused, scared, and has no idea of what's going on. Kelsey left without a word, and you're too damn wrapped up in your own misery to even think about anyone other than yourself." Her voice started to rise in volume.

Neil cringed as his headache went from a dull ache to a full-blown migraine.

"You're acting like a spoiled brat. I know it hurts, but you didn't give up when Rita died. Don't you dare roll over and die this time, just because Kelsey isn't here. Rikki needs her father more than ever right now, and you're a shit for brains for neglecting her."

"I'm not neglecting her —"

"Bullshit! You've been in here for the last two days without seeing her or talking to her, and you say that's not abandoning her?" She moved away.

Neil wondered if she was going to leave him alone.

Water ran in the sink for a moment.

"You had a fight with Kelsey? So what? Be a fucking man. Get off the floor, clean yourself up and be there for your daughter."

He shivered miserably as another icy waterfall slapped his face and upper body.

He rolled his eyes to the right, meeting her accusing deep blue stare.

She's right. He held out a hand to her. She helped him rise to his feet and kept her fingers on his elbow to steady him while she led him to the tub.

She sat him down on the side of it and crouched in front of him.

His chin sank to his chest, his shoulders slumped, and he shook from the dampness of his clothing and despair.

"Jesus, you're a mess." He could feel Ruby surveying his unshaven face, trembling hands, the black circles under his eyes, and his uneven breathing. "You look like you've been on a week-long drunk."

He chuckled hollowly. "I feel worse than that, more like the floor of a cheap taxi cab."

Her nose wrinkled. "You smell like it, too. Get in the shower while I get you some clean clothes. After that, you're going to shave, come out of this room, and have a good long talk with your daughter." Her voice had gentled a little.

"Hey, Ruby?" he asked as she started exiting the bathroom.

"Yeah?"

"Thanks. I needed the reminder that Rikki needs me too."

Neil followed Ruby's orders to the letter. He showered, shaved and dressed in the clothing Ruby left for him on his bed in haste, just so she wouldn't be yelling at him to hurry up every few minutes.

He found Rikki in the kitchen, crying on Gina's shoulder

while Taffy stuck close to her side.

Ruby sat at the table, with her eyes on the clock. "Good," she mouthed and glanced at his daughter.

Gina saw him and whispered something to Rikki.

She lifted her head, turned it to stare at him, and he could see his misery reflected in her tear-filled eyes. He held out his arms and she flew off the chair, into his embrace. He hugged her hard as she buried her face into his chest and started crying again.

A lump formed in Neil's throat and both shook in agony. "So sorry, sweetheart. I won't do that again."

"Where's Kelsey? I can't find her."

Neil whispered, "I don't know. We had a fight, and she left."

"She left without telling you why, or saying goodbye to me?" Rikki whimpered. "If she loves us so much, why did she do that?"

It felt like someone stabbed him and twisted the knife for extra agony. "It's her way," he murmured and tried not to let the dry heaves overtake him again.

Rikki's sobs increased in volume.

He squeezed her hard, and they let out their mutual agony and confusion.

CHAPTER FOURTEEN

On a dirt road a few miles west of Shelburne, Nova Scotia

The porch had separated from the side of rickety mobile home, and it sagged as the unpainted wood made a slow trip off of its moorings. The white metal siding was rusty, and there were a few spots that had corroded through the metal to show pink and yellow of the insulation underneath.

The lawn was brown, unkempt with its tall grass and weeds, and several small trees were growing in what was the path to the front door. The driveway was also grown over. There were no curtains in the windows.

Kelsey stared at her childhood home in shock. It was much worse than when she'd left almost thirteen years ago. She wondered how long it had been deserted. Maybe her mother had moved away — or had she died?

If her mother was dead, it meant she'd never get the chance to tell the rotten-hearted woman she had succeeded in life. Muriel would never know Kelsey was a good mother to her child, despite the beatings, the hateful words, and everything else Muriel Wagner had done or said to her daughter in those eighteen years.

Kelsey's gaze flickered around the sorry-looking property again. What was she doing here? She hadn't thought about her destination in her haste to get away from Neil and the pain of losing twelve years of her life with him.

"Hello?"

Her head whipped around to see an older lady standing by

her car's open window. Her memories faded.

"Are you lost?" the woman asked.

Kelsey shook her head. She glanced at the trailer and back to the lady.

"No one's lived there in over a year," the woman said with a mournful smile. "The last I heard, a distant cousin owns it now, but he lives out west and doesn't want the place. It's sad, really."

"Yeah," Kelsey murmured, wondering which cousin it was. She didn't know half of her relatives, thanks to her mother cutting herself off from her family when they had tried to get the child protective services after her for hurting Kelsey numerous times. That was over twenty years ago, and she had forgotten most of their names, and who was who in the family.

"Far as I know, the old woman that lived there is in some nursing home down around Clark's Harbour. I heard she has cancer and doesn't expect to live much longer." The lady eyed Kelsey and nodded. "Do you know her? You look a lot like her."

Kelsey let out a long breath and shook her head. "Nope, I'm just lost."

The woman shrugged. "Do you want directions back to the highway?"

Her mouth curled up in a friendly smile. "Sure, that would be great, thanks."

At her house the following night, after she finished her late evening shift, the argument with Neil rose to the top of her mind.

She sat in the shadows of her room, the only light visible in the crack where the streetlights peeked in between the gap in the drapes, and reflected on everything that had happened over the last year.

He knew how I felt back then, so why didn't he stay away and not try to stop it from happening after I moved out of the shelter? He wouldn't have been taking advantage of me, and he didn't say or do a damn thing other than let me fall completely in love with him.

I still can't understand why he started dating Rita if he cared about me so much. It was as if he was trying to prove something. But what was it? He must have loved her, else he wouldn't have married her and adopted Rikki.

She recalled the one time she had met the former Rita Hunter, and remembered how sweet and kind she had been during their short conversation.

When she found out the woman was dating Neil, it had hurt, so deeply that she felt her only option was to get away, so she wouldn't have to watch their affair with a smile on her face and her heart torn to shreds. She had run halfway across the country, hoping to get over him, and hadn't come back until he found her again, eleven years later.

Neil was the only person she couldn't cut out of her life for good. Her love for him was why she'd let him stay in touch with her, even if their communications had been sporadic and trickled off after a few years.

He was someone who believed in keeping in touch with those he cared about, and they'd had a good rapport, even after he started dating Rita. He'd always sent her updates on Rikki's progress and growth. His pride for his adopted child always made her smile, even if it hurt to remember how he was married to someone else.

Her head popped upwards and her eyes widened as his *Did he start dating Rita, even though she might have been second place in his heart, because he morally couldn't be with me?*

Her body froze in place.

What if I hadn't gone to Ontario? Would he have broken up with Rita in time?

Tears came into her eyes and her hand flew up to cover her mouth as the sobs began.

That's what he was trying to tell me. If I had stuck around, he might have ended it with her and told me how he really felt.

Jesus, I'm an idiot. No wonder he was so hurt when I got angry at him.

She wiped away the tears with the cuff of her hoodie sleeve and shook her head as shame rose.

Something within her solidified and replaced the guilt.

I needed a friend, and he was it. Even if we loved each other, we couldn't be together until I had healed and grew up a lot. He's almost fourteen years older than me. I was only eighteen when we met, still a kid, and he was over thirty.

What if my feelings had just been a case of loving the first person who had shown me any kindness, and who was trustworthy? We would have broken up and I would have hurt him.

I couldn't cut him out of my life, even to get over him.

I still can't do it. I love him too much to say goodbye to him.

I can't do it to Rikki either — she'll be heartbroken if I don't try to let things go and give her what she wants and needs. She needs her parents together, as a couple, not two sides of an ongoing war like so many kids have these days.

She leaned back in the chair with a soft smile and nodded.

She would close the door on her past and open wide the one to her future.

Tomorrow, on her day off.

Rikki is going to get her biggest wish.

Clark's Harbour
Nursing Home

Her footsteps echoed in the quiet of the hallway. Kelsey's stomach fluttered and her hands shook. Her nerves started to rise to the surface, and she determinedly took a deep, calming breath. The last thing she needed to show was fear or weakness during this final confrontation, and to crown the winner.

Her eyes located the room and she stopped a few feet away. Unwaveringly, she pulled out her compact to check her hair and makeup, then brushed a stray piece of lint off of her pale blue blouse, which was paired with a smart silver-grey suit and matching heels.

After deeming she was the image of perfection, Kelsey straightened to her full height, pushed her shoulders back, and held her head high as she knocked on the door.

An older nurse with greying hair and a kind smile opened it. "Yes?"

"I'm here to see Muriel, if she's awake," Kelsey replied.

Anxiety threatened to engulf her again when she heard a gritty yet familiar voice rasp, "Let whoever it is in, Danielle."

The nurse shrugged and slipped out to give them some privacy.

Kelsey swallowed hard and entered the room to face her mother for the last time.

"Well, who the hell are you?" the sunken, drawn body on the bed demanded as its beady eyes peered through beer-bottle-bottom glasses at her across the room.

Kelsey took a deep breath as a calming measure and walked toward the bed. "It's me, Mother," she replied, her voice steady.

Muriel Wagner narrowed her gaze as she surveyed Kelsey from top to bottom, from her clothing to her hair, and everything in between. "You're too damn high-classed looking to be my girl."

Kelsey gave her mother the same scrutiny, and started wondering why she had come. Was it to say goodbye, or rub her mother's nose in the fact that despite it all, she had succeeded?

She had loved her mother, even with the abuse and the booze.

Pity rose to overshadow the fear in her gut as she took in the withered body, sunken cheekbones, the balding scalp covered in a fine fuzz, and the wrinkled face covered in age spots.

Life hadn't been kind to Muriel.

Kelsey knew she didn't have to do anything to add to her mother's misery. The universe had done it for her.

She flipped a tendril of hair over her shoulder, and with a small smile, replied in a soft and strong voice, "It is me, Mother. I've changed a lot." She took a deep breath. "I've come by to let you know I'm going to be an author. Someone offered me a publishing deal, and I signed it. My book will be out later this year."

Muriel's expression didn't change, although there was a strange spark in her eyes.

"I also wanted to tell you that I'm getting married."

Her mother's eyebrows shot up. "I see."

"We haven't set a date yet, but we hope to do it soon."

Muriel nodded slowly. "Is he a nice man?"

Kelsey grinned. "The best. I'm also going to be a step-mother to his daughter."

Her mother absorbed it for a moment. "What's his name?"

"Neil."

"That's a nice, strong name," Muriel said with a nod. "Is he good to you?"

"Yes, he is."

"Then never be stupid like I was and ignore him, like I ignored your daddy," Muriel advised softly.

Kelsey blinked. It was the first admission her mother ever made about her mistakes and wrongdoings. "How so?" she asked.

Muriel sighed. "I loved boozing it up, getting into fights, and other men more than I loved him. I've had a lot of time to think over, and I've seen a few things I don't like about myself and what I was doing. If I had treated him better, he wouldn't have run off with that floozy."

Her hand reached out tentatively, and after hesitating for a moment, Kelsey took it. The skin was papery and somewhat cold, yet there was still a bit of strength left in it. It was a mother's touch, soft and affectionate.

Despite her initial shock over the gentleness behind it, Kelsey relaxed when she felt Muriel's other hand cover hers and squeeze her fingers.

It was the first time Kelsey remembered Muriel had touched her without any intent of hurt behind it.

"I made a lot of dumb mistakes in my time," her mother continued, "and girl, if you make the same ones, it would be my fault, because I treated you like dirt. No kid deserves that. I didn't know how to treat you right, because my mom died when I was a baby, and my daddy beat the shit out of me every day, too. I thought I could do better than him, and I messed up."

Her lips curled upwards. "You're going to be an author, married to a good man, and you're going to be a great stepmom to that girl of his, aren't you?"

Kelsey nodded and tears prickled her eyes. "I hope so."

"No, just do it," Muriel ordered, "and never let the shit I did to you ruin you or your family. Understand?"

Kelsey grinned tearfully. "Yes, ma'am." It was only order from her mother that she was going to happily follow to the letter.

"I'm glad you came by. I'm not going to live much longer — cancer."

Kelsey nodded. "I'm sorry about that."

"Ain't nothing I don't deserve, after all the mean things I did in life." She peered up at her daughter. "You to go back to your Neil and that little girl, and do me proud, Kelsey Bernice. Never look back."

"I won't."

"Be good. I did love you."

Kelsey nodded and a tear leaked out of her eye. She whispered, "I forgive you."

Her mother gave her a tearful smile and replied, "No need for any of that, I'm not worth it. Just go home, hold your man tight and that little girl even tighter. Never look back."

Kelsey gave her mother's hand one last squeeze, and knew it would be the last time they saw each other. Without thinking, she gave the papery skin of Muriel's cheek a quick kiss and whispered, "Goodbye, Mother."

Her mother patted her hand once more, and with determination and peace surrounding her, Kelsey walked out.

The outside door of the garage stood open to let in the early summer breeze, and Punky was taking advantage of it to run around Neil as he vacuumed the interior of his car.

"Chowder head, put that down," he ordered as Punky grabbed the brush attachment with his jaws.

The corgi skidded between his legs, and Neil almost went face first into the open car door.

"Idiot!" he yelled at Punky's retreating hindquarters.

The dog had been naughty lately, and the cats had been worse. He had found several heaps of dog poop and hacked up hairballs around the house, and several items of his had been either shredded by sharp feline claws or ripped apart by canine teeth.

Neil understood. Like him and Rikki, they were missing a part of their family, and the only way they could express it was by behaving badly. Unlike their human counterparts, they couldn't let out their grief by crying. They knew he was the blame, and they took it out on him.

He had cried a lot in the three days since Kelsey's silent exit, with Rikki, or alone, and had cursed his big mouth several times over the long hours during the darkest part of the night.

His throat closed as Kelsey's accusations of being afraid of their feelings for each other and why he hadn't acted upon them rang in his ears.

"Don't think about that," he muttered and picked up the hose and turned on the vacuum.

Despite his verbal reminder, their history went through his mind again as he meticulously went over every inch of the back seat and floor. He let it flow and used the mundane chore to mull it over. He analyzed his feelings for her, the reasons why he hadn't followed his heart in the beginning, his true reasons for marrying Rita though she was a distant second to Kelsey, and everything else.

He was cleaning the back of the driver's seat when Punky tore past him toward the garage door with an excited bark.

Startled, Neil banged his head on the interior's roof and let out a loud curse as stars popped in front of his eyes. "Get back here, you jackass!" he bellowed, and backed out of the car to chase the dog.

When he straightened, his gaze landed on the silhouette of a person standing at the threshold, on the gravel of the drive-way. Their face was hidden by the glare of the sun behind them, and he squinted to dispel the dazzle. Whoever it was, they were female, going by the shape, and hope started to rise.

He squashed it with a firm reminder that it could be Ruby or Gina checking up on them, and turned back to his task, while glancing at the other person out of the corner of his eye.

She stepped into the cool shadows of the garage, and the vacuum's hose slipped from fingers numbed with shock to clatter upon the floor when his gaze met hers.

"Hey," Kelsey whispered awkwardly and shoved her hands into her jean pockets.

Her words snapped his disbelief. He broke eye contact and angrily grabbed the hose from the floor. Without looking at her, he said quietly, "What are you doing here?"

She took a tentative step toward him. "I'm, uh, here to—

Christ." She sighed and kicked at the floor with a sneaker.

He tapped the nozzle on his free hand and agony flooded him. "If you're here for your stuff and the cats, just do it so we can get this over with. You're itching to shut the door, so don't make it any more painful than it is already."

Leave me alone, Kelsey. Please. I'm dying inside. The longer you stay, the more it hurts.

Kelsey straightened to her full height. "Do you really think that's why I'm here?"

He scoffed. "Once you walk away, there's no turning back. When you're done, it's forever."

"You were the exception to that rule."

"I made you promise you'd keep in touch."

She took another step toward him. Neil stiffened in a warning to stay back, but she kept coming closer until she was on the opposite side of the door from him, close enough to touch.

"I would have done it anyway," she replied and put her hand on the top of the car door. "I wanted to talk to you, no matter how far we lived apart, even after you married Rita. I really cared about you. I couldn't let go of that tiny bit of hope that someday–" She averted her gaze.

His hand fisted around the hose as zaps of pain hit every one of his nerve endings. "You got what you wanted, and it was your choice to walk away, then and now. Stop wasting my time," he snapped before he turned on the vacuum to shut her out.

She flipped it off a second later. "Neil, at least hear what I have to say."

He glared at her. "You're going to give a speech before you run this time? Wow, I must be special if you're going to do that," he muttered sarcastically and turned the vacuum on again.

It died a few seconds later, and when he touched the switch, it didn't whirl into action.

"Try starting it without the damn thing being plugged in,"

Kelsey muttered and dangled the plug in his face.

He tried to snatch it out of her hand and cursed when she yanked it away. "Give it back."

"After I'm done telling you what I've come to say." She shoved the plug down the back of her jeans and folded her arms across her chest with a smug look.

He glowered at her. If that was how she wanted it, fine, he'd let her do it, and hoped her deathblow was fast. The agony of losing her was too much for him. The slower it was, the more it would hurt.

He leaned against the side of the car and muttered, "Get it over with before Rikki sees you. If she knows you're here and why, it'll break her heart. Consider yourself a dead woman if that happens."

Her smile snapped into desolation as his words slapped her.

His smile was sarcastic. "Didn't think about *my* daughter, did you?"

"I thought she might have been at Taffy's house," Kelsey whispered. She raised her gaze to his. "And she's *our* daughter."

"She's mine. You made that very clear when you took off without even letting her know where you were going or saying goodbye to her," Neil bellowed painfully.

Kelsey winced. "I forgot my phone and —" she whispered and tears filled her eyes.

"That's what you get for rushing out of here like hell was on your heels."

"I was upset!"

"You caused a hell of a lot of pain when you walked out on us without looking back."

"I wasn't walking out on you and Rikki, Neil," she cried around a sob. "I was going to go to the beach, calm down and come back to talk to you, but when I got in the car, I just drove and kept going. I didn't come out of it until I was in Lockport, three hours later. If I had returned then, we would have had a bigger fight, in front of Rikki."

"You should have come back then. I wouldn't be this mad if you had."

The flat of her hand slammed against the door's window with a loud crack. "Maybe I had a few things to do before I came back."

"Yeah, like what? You could have done them after we talked, I would have understood."

"It was stuff I had to do on my own, and if I had told you what I was up to, you would have zoomed down there on a white charger, to do it for me!" she shot back and threw her arms wide. "Neil Falcon, the savior of the lost, would have taken over and never let me get over my past and everything else."

"I'm not a savior of lost souls. I would have stood back and supported you while you were—Jesus." He back-kicked the fender and stomped a few steps away to cool his temper and get a grip on his pain, while he hoped she would leave.

She didn't move, and Neil wondered if it was to prolong the agony.

"I threw out my birth control pills," she blurted.

"What does that have to do with you leaving?" he asked over his shoulder.

"Remember how I told you I was going to get my tubes tied, and you talked me out of it?"

"I remember," he replied and wondered what prompted her to do that.

"I stayed on them even after we started dating. I thought Rikki was enough for us, but I'm not so sure she should be our only child."

He slowly turned around and stared at her. Tears poured out of her eyes and she shook as she hugged herself around her stomach.

Hope rose when his gaze met hers, and he saw his despair mirrored in her eyes. "Kelsey, what do you mean by she shouldn't be *our* only child?"

"I want another baby sometime, but only if you're the father."

"What?" he asked incredulously.

She took a deep breath. "I'm not running. I *can't* run from you," she choked out between sobs. "You were right about me needing time to heal, to grow up and put everything behind me before we could be together. I was stupid to think we had a lot of wasted years, when we really didn't.

"I was so pissed off at you for marrying Rita. I wanted to hate both of you for breaking my heart, but I couldn't. Rita was so nice to me, and if it hadn't been for her, you wouldn't have adopted Rikki. I was sad to hear she died, but if she hadn't, you wouldn't have found out the truth about Rikki's birth, or how I was her biological mother."

Neil nodded. "She led me back to you, even if she didn't know it," he said quietly.

"That's why I can't hate her. She didn't steal you from me, she was the catalyst that caused Rikki and me to know each other, and for me to see that I'm not a terrible person or mother after all. I owe her one, because she gave me the two best things in my life, you and Rikki." Her sobs turned to gasps and she covered her face with her hands.

"I needed to put away my past so I could start our future, and I had to do it alone. I didn't want to scare you, or make you think I was breaking up with you, Neil. I'm so sorry, and I want to stay, but if you want me to go, I'll do it."

"Kelsey, look at me."

She raised her head and stared at him across six feet of cement floor.

"I'm sorry too, sweetheart. I shouldn't have let things go as far as they did back then, but no matter how many times I tried staying away, I couldn't. You were too important to me, and although it broke my heart to do it, I thought what I did was for the best, for both of us at the time. Being your friend was better than nothing, and I needed you in my life, somehow."

"I forgive you," she whispered, "I'll always forgive you, no matter what. I love you."

Neil closed his eyes as joy and relief rose in his chest. "Kelsey, come here." He held out his arms, and hugged her when she flew into his embrace.

Their mouths met softly and between kisses, he murmured, "I'll always forgive you, too. I love you too damn much to let go of you, got it?"

"Got it," she choked out and snuggled closer to him. "Never scare me like that again, please."

"I won't, and if your offer is still there, let's do it."

He pulled back to stare down at her oddly. "Do what?"

She grinned tearfully. "Get that damn license, and see a Justice of the Peace, so I can finally say I'm Mrs. Neil Falcon."

Joy and pride shot up his spine and he kissed her.

"Dad, are you down there?" Rikki's voice echoed from above.

He turned his head toward the stairwell. "Yeah, I'm here," he called.

Punky zoomed down ahead of Rikki with an excited yap and his bum wiggling.

"Chowder head was barking at the front door, and I thought you left without putting him inside."

A tread on the top stair signaled they wouldn't be alone much longer.

A pair of sock-covered feet appeared, and after another two steps downward, their daughter poked her head out from under the ledge.

"What are you doing here?" she demanded and glared at her mother.

Kelsey exchanged a glance with Neil.

His arms tightened around Kelsey as he explained, "Your mother came back to apologize."

"And you believed her, after what she did?" Rikki snapped tearfully.

"I didn't mean to run off like that without telling you, or saying goodbye. That was stupid of me, and it's never going to happen again," Kelsey explained.

"How do we know that? You could have another big fight with Dad."

"I'll be fighting to stay, and for your father and you! I love both of you too much," Kelsey shot back around a sob. "You and your dad are my entire life. No more running."

Rikki stopped crying and stared at her blankly with wide eyes.

"Kelsey agreed to marry me, and like me, doesn't believe in divorce," Neil added quietly with a half-smile. "I don't think we have to worry about her taking off again, now that she knows she's loved and wanted, just as much as she loves and wants both of us in her life."

"Rikki, your dad and I won't get married without your approval. You're a package deal. One doesn't come without the other."

The girl raised an eyebrow at them as she considered it.

"Come on, Erika, don't you want to give me a chance to be a step-mom to you?" Kelsey asked.

A slow grin started to form on Rikki's face as she straightened and ambled her way down the stairs. She stopped by her parents and with a nod, said, "Okay."

Kelsey and Neil pulled her into their embrace to form a family unit. He hugged both of them, tightly.

Rikki snuggled closer to her parents.

"Kelsey?" Rikki asked after a minute.

"Yeah?"

"You're not my step-mom, you're my mom."

She sniffled and kissed Rikki's temple. "My baby." She lifted her face to stare up at him. Neil's heart skipped a beat when he saw the adoration in her eyes. "My love."

Neil grinned as he stared into the loving gaze of the woman he had loved for over a decade and whispered, "My girls."

They kissed softly, and Kelsey rested her head on his shoulder. "I'm never letting go of either of you again."

Thank god, Neil thought as he hugged Rikki to his side and kissed his new fiancée.

The End

ACKNOWLEDGEMENTS:

Thank you to my long-time friend Dawn B. for allowing me to pick her brain and for sharing her knowledge about the Pembroke Welsh Corgi. Her dogs Sensei, Lucy and Tucker are the inspiration for Rikki's dog, Punky.

You may also enjoy the following from eXtasy Books Inc:

Striken
V.J. Allison

Excerpt

An hour later, Ewan managed to drag Shannon out of the bar.

Although he was starting to feel the effects of drinking six bottles of beer in less than ninety minutes, he managed to walk out of his friends' sight without showing he was on the verge of being unsteady, or making a bigger fool out of himself.

Shannon stewed for the entire taxi ride back to his condominium.

With a sniff, she pouted the instant the main door was locked behind them.

"Your friends hate me."

Ewan rubbed a hand down his face in frustration. No matter what he said, she was going to have a tantrum and play the victim instead of taking responsibility for her nasty behaviour.

Fine with him. He was in the mood for a fight, and his humiliation at her hands added to the urge to put her in her place.

"Maybe if you talked to them instead of down to them, they would have liked you."

"What's that supposed to mean?"

He didn't reply as he turned and walked unsteadily into the kitchen. His jacket landed on a chair at the breakfast bar, and a cupboard slammed open.

Shannon walked into the area just as he turned the cap off a bottle of scotch.

"I said, what's that supposed to mean?" Her tone suggested she was getting angry.

Good.

"You acted like you were the queen and they were your subjects," Ewan replied and took a long swig of the amber liquid.

Her eyes started to bulge, an indication she was building up to a tantrum. "I didn't do anything! That nasty bitch Karla flew into me for no reason!"

"Her name is Kara, and I don't blame her for flying into you after you asked her if she mucked out stables for a living! She has a fucking doctorate in psychology, that's a long way from scooping shit out of a paddock."

"How was I supposed to know?" she moaned, and folded her arms across her chest. The action caused her dress to ride up her thighs to show she wasn't wearing any panties under the skintight material. Her hairless mound shined softly in the muted light of the kitchen, and a shudder of revulsion crawled up his spine as he stared at her.

It was akin to what a hooker would wear as she prowled the streets, looking for johns.

For the first time, Ewan realized how little class Shannon had, even though she worked in the higher end of the realty market.

An image of Marti's white turtleneck, hockey jersey and semi-faded blue jeans rose in his mind as he stared at his current girlfriend.

Marti always looked like a lady, even when she wasn't

wearing anything . . .

Another long gulp of scotch burned its way down his throat. Anger fuelled his need to drink himself into a stupor, and forget this night ever happened. How he was going to face his coworkers on Monday, Ewan wasn't sure, and it was all thanks to Shannon.

"You've been in therapy, that's how you're supposed to know. Psychologists are the same pretty much right across the country, and you insulted not one, but two of them tonight!"

She pouted again, which set his temper into the stratosphere. Ewan slammed the bottle down on the counter in disgust and snarled, "Maybe if you had actually listened instead of assumed or ignored what they were saying, they would have liked you."

She ignored his last remark and sashayed over to him. "You didn't have a good time tonight, did you? I'm sorry. How's about I make you feel better?" Coiling her body around his, she ran her tongue along his neck, and moved her hand from his stomach to his belt.

Even with the alcohol starting to affect his senses and reason, Ewan could still see her play to manipulate him into forgiving her rudeness toward his friends and coworkers.

His eyes blazed with ferocity as he grabbed her hand and moved it away from him. "This is exactly what I mean," he hissed icily. "You were rotten to everyone else, and you tried having sex with me in front of the entire bar." Another image, one of Marti's disgusted and distantly cool stare, overlaid his vision and added to his anger. "What in the hell were you thinking? You never acted like that before. It was embarrassing, and disgusting!"

With a loud curse, he yanked his body away from hers and stumbled toward the hallway. He almost lost his balance and halfway to his bedroom, he had to stop and lean against the wall.

He felt clumsy and his mind was hazy, from the effects of the booze combined with his anger at Shannon. He kept seeing the detached look on Marti's face as she watched Shannon acting like a bitch in heat, and heard the echoes of the disdain in her voice when he was sticking up for her.

His eyes squeezed shut and his hands reached up to fist in his hair as the uninvited memories from his time with her flashed through his mind.

An image of Marti writhing beneath him in the midst of an orgasm lingered longer than the rest, and his body reacted with an unwelcome and painful arousal.

Ewan didn't feel the hands on his belt, nor did he hear the loud rasp of a zipper being pulled down. The only thing he was conscious of was a short blast of cool air on his flesh, followed by a wet heat that coiled bliss around him. Pleasure shot up his length and his head fell back to rest against the wall. His breath came in short pants, and he unconsciously reached down to hold the warmth in place as he thrust his hips forward.

His drunken haze shattered when his fingers tangled in short spikes instead of long, silky strands. When his eyes flew open and he saw Shannon kneeling in front of him, his hardness turned flaccid. Bile rose in his throat.

A quick and clumsy twist of his body made her let go.

Surprise made her lose her balance and fall to her backside as she stared up at him with wide eyes.

"You know I don't like it when you do that. Now get up and get out."

She leaped to her feet and her hand was a blur. "Asshole! You wanted a blow job!"

Ewan caught it a bare inch from his face.

He had to get away from her before he hit her, even in self-defence.

"Go home, Shannon," he slurred wearily and dropped her hand as he turned away.

"I don't have to listen to you!"

"Get out of here before I get up in the morning, or I'll call the cops. It's your choice."

He left her sputtering in shock as he stumbled into his bedroom and locked the door.

ABOUT THE AUTHOR

V.J. Allison was born and raised in southern Nova Scotia, Canada, and her work reflects her strong Maritime roots. She is a stay-at-home mother to a son on the autism spectrum, married to the love of her life, and "mama" to a rescued Maine Coon cat named Marnie.

She has been writing various stories of novel length and short stories since her school days, and sees writing as a vital component to her life.

When she isn't writing, she loves to read romance and science fiction novels (notably Star Wars); listen to music (heavy metal, rock, alternative); watch various crime and forensic dramas; watch science fiction television shows and movies; and spend time with her large family and many friends.

This self-proclaimed geeky rocker chick is a warrior and advocate for various chronic illnesses including Occipital Neuralgia, Trigeminal Neuralgia, Diabetes, Migraines, and Glossopharyngeal Neuralgia. She is also an advocate for the prevention of animal cruelty and is a voice for Autism Awareness.

Her first book, *Stricken*, was released by eXtasy Books on March 17, 2017, and has garnered positive reviews.

https://vjallison.com